Call of the Blood

Beautiful young Cat Falcon knew of her birthright long before she ever set eyes on the ancient manor of Kingsmead and the horror-haunted family whose name and blood she shared.

Exiled to distant Wales by those who wished to disown her, Cat was raised by a woman who told her of the dazzling splendor and sinister evil of the Falcon past, and of the dangers of ever attempting to demand her Falcon legacy.

But already Cat bore on her thigh the strange purple crescent that was the Falcon mark of the occult. Already her mind was prey to visions of the hidden past and the mysterious future. And already her body and her soul were ripening toward the day when she would have to return to Kingsmead in perilous disguise to battle against fiendish betrayal and forbidden passion in the climactic struggle for the Falcon fate. . . .

THE FALCON SAGA *by Catherine Darby*

All available exclusively from Popular Library

Catherine Darby's
The Falcon Saga - 9
Falcon Sunset

POPULAR LIBRARY • NEW YORK

POPULAR LIBRARY EDITION
November, 1976

ISBN: 0-445-00420-7

PRINTED IN THE UNITED STATES OF AMERICA

THE FALCONS

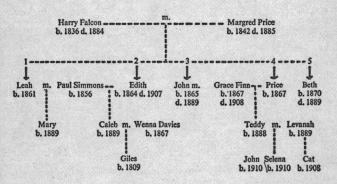

Harry Falcon
b. 1836 d. 1884

— m. —

Margred Price
b. 1842 d. 1885

1 — 2 — 3 — 4 — 5

Leah
b. 1861 — m. — Paul Simmons
b. 1856

Edith
b. 1864 d. 1907

John m.
b. 1865
d. 1889

Grace Finn — Price
b. 1867 b. 1867
d. 1908

Beth
b. 1870
d. 1889

Mary
b. 1889

Caleb m. Wenna Davies
b. 1889 b. 1867

Teddy m. Levanah
b. 1888 b. 1889

Giles
b. 1809

John Selena Cat
b. 1910 b. 1910 b. 1908

Chapter 1

1916

Twilight had purpled the grass and the greening apples hung heavily on the gnarled trees. Both the cows had been milked and the pony fed and watered, the fire built up for the evening and the dishes washed.

Cat Falcon, swinging to and fro on the white painted gate, glanced back at Saron Farm with a look of almost maternal pride. She had, as usual, performed all her tasks carefully and now was taking a little time in which to be a child. At eight she wore too often the look of an adult weighed down by responsibility, but at this moment her round face was innocent of anxiety, her green eyes sparkling, her black plaits flopping up and down against her back. Although she was small for her age she was wiry, her wrists strong as steel, her narrow shoulders held proudly in readiness for any burden. Wind and sun had tanned her skin to pale copper and her voice raised in tuneless humming was sweet and soulless as that of a bird.

Opposite her the fields slipped away toward the range of mountains that rose up in the blue air. Cat had never been beyond those hills, had never been out of Wales in her life. Indeed the farthest she had ever been in Wales was only on a day trip to Rhyl. Some of the local children had been taken in a charabanc to the seaside. There had been sticky buns and lemonade and the salty tang of sea on her lips. The others had run about, tossing a colored ball and rolling their wooden hoops, but Cat had stood very quietly at the fringe of the white-tipped waves and watched a brown seaweed trail lazy fingers under the water.

She had told Aunt Catrin about it and the old woman had smiled and said it sounded grand and exciting, and then, in the middle of saying it, had fallen asleep. Falling asleep was a habit with Aunt Catrin, but she was past ninety and not as spry as she had been. Once or twice she had begun to tell Cat who she really was and who her family had been and then broken off, saying there was time enough for that.

But of late she had grown more slow in her movements, more apt to fall asleep in the middle of a sentence. Cat, looking at her through the unsentimental eyes of a child, decided that she had better find out what she wanted to know before Aunt Catrin forgot real life altogether and drifted into a perpetual sleep.

The child had drifted into a half-dream herself, the road blurring as she swung lazily to and fro, one foot on the lowest bar of the gate, the other propelling her from the new-swept yard.

A scene, vivid as reality, was forming behind her eyes. Men stumbled through mud that sucked at their boots. A horse, belly distended, lay on its back with its legs sticking up into smoke-darkened air. There was a constant rumbling interspersed with sharp cracks of rifle fire. Two soldiers came into view, the one leaning on the other. Their grimed faces bore a strong family resemblance and one appeared to be half-carrying the other, but the noise around them was so intense that she could not distinguish any words that passed between them. Then came a rattle of shots and, above them, the man supporting his companion screamed out, "I'm hit, Teddy! I'm hit!" and the whole scene was swallowed up in red-streaked dust.

Cat, her head throbbing, clung to the gate. The country road that wound toward Caernarvon came back into view, the mountains tranquil in the distance. She had known such experiences before and accepted them as an unpleasant fact of life, but this one had been more horrifying than most.

She shut the gate abruptly and ran across the yard to the stone-built cottage. Saron was more of a small holding than a farm, but it provided a livelihood for Aunt Catrin and herself. It had never occurred to her to regard the house as small or shabby. She had been born in the cottage and reared there by Aunt Catrin, who had been her great-great-grandmother's sister. That much she had been told already.

The big living room that stretched from front to back of the building was warm and cheerful. Aunt Catrin glanced up as the child appeared and blinked. Her eyes were no longer as sharp as they had been, but she resented having to wear spectacles.

"Have you done your tasks, cariad?" she inquired.

"Aunt Catrin, are there men fighting somewhere?" Cat asked.

"In France," the old woman nodded. "But it's a

long way off, and not for a little girl to bother her head about."

"Who are fighting?"

"The Germans are fighting the English and the French. There's a war on."

"Is somebody called Teddy fighting in the war?" Cat asked.

"Teddy?" The old woman's voice sharpened.

"What did it mean?" Cat asked. Her eyes, large,

"I saw it." The child sat down on the stool at Aunt Catrin's knee. "I had one of my seeing times just now. There was mud and the firing of guns, and two soldiers one carrying the other, and the one who was carrying called out, 'I'm hit, Teddy! I'm hit!' I didn't see any more."

The old woman looked down at the child thoughtfully. The two of them were very close but there was much that she had not told, partly because the girl was too little to understand the complexities of human relationships, and partly because some part of her own nature wanted to keep the girl's affections to herself.

"What did it mean?" Cat asked. Her eyes, large, slanting and emerald, were fixed upon the wrinkled countenance.

"Some folk are born with the seeing in their eyes," Aunt Catrin said.

"Like when Mair Pritchard was wed, and I cried because I saw her lying with flowers all about her?"

"And she died of her firstborn within the twelve-month," Aunt Catrin said, nodding.

"And is it bad?" Cat asked. "Is it bad to have the seeing times?"

"Uncomfortable," said the old woman, leaning to unplait the thick braids. "It's a gift, they say. I'd call it a curse myself. It runs in families. My sister Saran had a touch of it, and a mark on her leg just as you have."

Cat tugged up her red flannel skirt and examined the purple crescent etched deeply into her thigh.

"It's the mark of a witch," she said, half proudly, half afraid. "Huw the Fish told me that. He said it was the devil's kiss."

"Huw the Fish can keep his opinions to himself!" Aunt Catrin said testily.

"Aunt Catrin?" The little girl jerked her head away from the gnarled fingers, and twisted around on the stool.

"What is it, Cat?"

"Who was my mother?" the child asked. "Who was she, Aunt Catrin? My second name is Falcon, isn't it? Was she Mrs. Falcon?"

Aunt Catrin sighed, her hand dropping to her lap. "Your mother's name is Levanah," she said at last. "Levanah Falcon. She was never wed and she never told me who your father was. She came here one day and told me she was going to have a baby. She was my sister's great-granddaughter so I took her in. After you were born she went away into England again."

"Didn't she want me?" Cat asked.

"You must try to understand," Aunt Catrin said. "Levanah was born in England, in Kent, at a big house called Kingsmead. She was reared there with her cousins, Mary and Teddy—"

"Teddy?"

"After you were born she went back and married Teddy," Aunt Catrin went on. "You know, I was married once and had a little girl."

"Like me?"

"She had green eyes like you, but her hair was brown," the old woman remembered. "I was past forty when she was born, and when she was a young woman she went away into England too, to live with her Falcon relatives. She married one of the Falcons and never came back to Wales, but she still writes to me every Christmas and sends money when she can."

"And my mother is alive? All this time alive and never coming?"

"She went back into England. That side of the family, the Falcon side, never knew she'd had a child. My own daughter Wenna doesn't know."

"I'm a secret then," said Cat.

"A special secret," said Aunt Catrin.

Cat was quiet, considering. She had always known herself to be different, because of the seeing times. Now it seemed that she was different in another way.

"Tell me about them," she urged. "Tell me about the Falcons."

"My own mother was one," Aunt Catrin said. "She was the daughter of Apple Falcon who lies over in the pasture with a stone above her."

"Next to her husband," Cat said.

"My mother went into England when she was a girl and wed one of her Falcon cousins," said Aunt Catrin. "But she came back here to the farm and my sister and I were born. We were twins and she never told us who our father was, save it was not her husband. After she died we lived together, Saran and I. She was a gentle dark thing with no sense in her head and one day a traveling man stopped by and she lay down under the apple trees for him."

"Did she have a baby?" Cat, to whom the mysteries of reproduction were part of everyday life on the farm, looked up with interest.

"And died of it. I reared my niece, Margred, as I reared you, but I was young then. I took a husband and we lived here, the three of us, until Margred went into England to seek her Falcon cousins. She married one of them and had a big family, and never came back. I had my own child then, and my husband died, and Wenna left and married a Falcon too. I've had news of them over the years, but I never laid eyes on any of them till Margred's granddaughter walked in one day and went away again after you were born."

"And the Falcons? Tell me about them."

"Cariad, I never met any of them," said the old woman. "My own Wenna married Cal Falcon. Then there was Mary, and Teddy, who wed your mother. They have twins, but I can't remember their names."

"I would like to meet them," Cat said. "I would like to go into England and meet them."

"Nothing but hurt ever came from going into England," Aunt Catrin said. "Far better for you to stay here with me."

"My mother might be pleased to see me," Cat argued. "She might be surprised."

"She'd be surprised, I grant you," Aunt Catrin said dryly. "She told me long ago to put you in an orphanage."

"But you kept me."

"Because I wanted something young about the place," the old woman said. "I wanted someone for company. Everything here dies or goes into England."

"I won't go into England until after you're dead," Cat promised earnestly.

"And not even then if you've any sense," said Aunt Catrin. "I've willed the farm to you, and you'd do well to marry a nice local boy and settle here."

Cat smiled without answering. She was trying to work out how many more years Aunt Catrin might be expected to live. It was not that she wished the old woman any harm but it would be interesting to go to England and meet these Falcon relatives and see the mother who wished to put her in an orphanage.

The apple logs in the hearth spluttered and wound sweet-smelling mist into the air. At the heart of the scarlet flames the outlines of a big, gabled house took shape. Cat narrowed her eyes but the house was crumbling into ash and there was no more to be seen.

Aunt Catrin had nodded off to sleep, a gentle snore occasionally escaping her parted lips. It was odd to think of her as having once been young. She had been a big woman with red hair, but had bent with the years, her hair whitening, her freckled skin shrinking against her bones.

Cat rose and padded into the bedroom. There were two bedrooms, one behind the other, leading off the main living room. Her own, like the one in which Aunt Catrin slept, had whitewashed walls and rag rugs on the floor. Under the window a chest held her clothes, and on the high dresser were the three objects that had been there as long as she could remember.

She reached up now and lifted them down one by one, placing them on the floor and squatting before them, with her legs tucked under her skirt, her loosened braids swinging down at each side of her little face.

She studied the objects carefully, wondering why, though they were so different, they seemed to belong together. The crystal ball of opaque greenish glass, the tiny wooden figure of a man playing a pipe, a portrait showing the head and shoulders of a girl.

She had always understood that her mother had brought the things to Saron. Aunt Catrin had told her once that the girl in the picture was Cat's grandmother, who had died young. Her name had been Beth. The name suited her, Cat thought. There was a quietness about it, and a quietness in the round face and eyes of the girl in the picture. Beth had had golden-brown hair and eyes that were a mixture of many tints, and on one hand gleamed a ring set with a blue-white stone.

Other children had imaginary playmates when they grew lonely. Cat had always talked to the girl in the picture and sometimes it seemed that the girl was about to reply, the lips parting, the eyes ready to flash with laughter or tears.

"I'm going over into England one day," Cat whispered, "and find my mother. She will have a big surprise when she meets me, won't she?"

The face stared back at her, the moonstone glinting on the hand.

Cat turned to the little carved figure. It sat on its base of wood, cross-legged, its mouth curved up into a grin, its eyes half closed in pleasure, its head crowned by a pointed cap fringed with tiny wooden leaves. She stroked it with her forefinger, enjoying the warmth of the rough-grained wood. Her mother had left that at Saron too, together with the crystal.

Between her narrow palms the glass ball was

smooth and cool and heavy. She gazed into it, watching the surface grow cloudy, watching the tiny spark of light swim up from the milky depths and increase to a brightness into which she was drawn.

The house was there again, but within a moment she realized it was not the same building but a much smaller one with trees around it. The house was of whitewashed stone with small, bright windows. It seemed to be empty but, as she watched, a figure moved to the door and stood gazing out across uncut grass and white-starred bushes. The figure was that of a young girl, with a tail of honey-colored hair over one shoulder and a blue-white ring on the finger of one hand. She had a green dress with a white sailor collar, and she held her head to one side as if she were listening. But there was no sound except the murmuring of water somewhere beyond the trees. Then the girl began to weep, silently and copiously, the tears rolling down her cheeks. She put up her hands in a clumsy, childish gesture, and Cat saw there were red bands around her wrists. Even as she watched the bands began to drip red drops onto the white collar and the drops joined into a thin stream of scarlet that splashed into an ever widening pool at her feet. The round face grew paler and paler, the edges of the figure beginning to blur, the rushing of the river becoming so loud that it drowned even the thoughts in Cat's own head.

The child was whirled back, sobbing, into the bedroom. Her legs were cramped, her fingers tightly clenched around the glass ball. Tears splashed onto her wrists and the sun, sinking into the west, cast a red shadow over her.

"Cariad, are you all right?" said Aunt Catrin from the doorway.

"I had another seeing time," Cat whispered. "I saw a little house and a girl bleeding."

"You ought not to go looking into that crystal," Aunt Catrin scolded. "Nasty, heathen thing!"

"The girl bleeding was my mother's mother," Cat said. "She was the one called Beth. The one in the picture, Auntie."

"It was a dream you dreamed," said the old woman soothingly. "You spend too much time by yourself. It will be better when school starts again."

"I don't like school," Cat sniffed, wrinkling her nose.

"But you must learn to read and write and count," Aunt Catrin urged. "When you're a big girl you'll want to be going to the County School."

"Witches don't go to school," Cat said obstinately.

"And that's enough of that! I'll have a word to say to Huw the Fish when I catch him," the old woman said crossly. "Now put those things away and dry your eyes."

"I was thinking about my mother," Cat said. "She didn't want me, did she? Was I a very ugly baby?"

"You were a very pretty one, like a little doll."

"Then why didn't she want me?" the child asked. "Why did she just go away and leave me? Didn't she care what happened to me?"

"Why, of course she cared!" Aunt Catrin sounded angry. "She cared very much and she was very sad that she couldn't take you back to her family. She left something for you, something for you to have when you are older."

"What is it?" Cat, on tiptoe to replace the little wooden figure, looked eager. "Can I see it now?"

"I suppose there's no harm in your seeing it," Aunt Catrin said doubtfully. "Wait while I get it from my room." She shuffled out, her expression one of concern. Cat, having put back the three objects, sniffed again, tears drying up in anticipation of what might be to come.

Aunt Catrin returned and held out her hand in silence. On the curved palm a ring gleamed, the stone blue-white.

"It belonged to Beth, to your grandmother," she said. "Beth was the youngest of my niece Margred's children. She wore the ring and after she died it went to her daughter, Levanah. She gave it to me to keep for you."

The ring was loose on Cat's finger. She transferred it to her thumb and admired it.

"It's a moonstone," said Aunt Catrin. "On the day Our Lord was crucified the moon fairies wept and each of their tears became a moonstone."

"The girl Beth was crying," Cat said. "She was crying and bleeding. I saw her."

"You were dreaming," Aunt Catrin said again. "Give me the ring. You can wear it when you're older."

Reluctantly Cat drew the jewel from her thumb and gave it back.

"I'll make a cup of tea and you can have it in bed like a princess," Aunt Catrin said. "You'd like that, wouldn't you? And I'll tell you a fairy story, or we'll sing some of the old tunes together."

She looked hopefully at the small girl, trying with her words to draw a circle of safe, familiar life about them both.

"That will be nice," Cat said politely, but her own gaze was veiled.

She had a mother called Levanah who had married a cousin called Teddy. A man called Teddy was fighting in France. Her mother lived in a big house called Kingsmead, and she had been sad not to be able to take Cat there. Instead she had left her the moonstone ring that had belonged to her own mother, to the girl in the portrait who had cried and stood, bleeding, at the door of a little white cottage.

Thoughts jumbled in her mind as she pulled off her bodice and skirt and wriggled into the white nightdress with featherstitching at neck and wrists. Aunt Catrin's eyes and hands were not equal to the task of sewing, but Megan Jones from town made good quality garments cheaply, and thanks to her skill Cat was always nicely dressed.

The room was growing rapidly dimmer and cooler. The day had been warm and bright, but now there came a spatter of rain against the window and pale ghost mist made patterns beyond the glass.

"Get into bed now, cariad," the old woman said, coming back with a tray. "There are two cups of tea for us, and some bara-brith. You'd like a little supper now to settle you."

Cat nodded and climbed up into the big bed with its feather mattress and woven quilt, plumping the pillow behind her. The tea, only slightly slopped into the saucer, was black and sweet as she and Aunt Catrin liked it. She sank her teeth into the thickly buttered currant bread and made her eyes big with appreciation.

"What story would you like?" Aunt Catrin asked, preparing to search her memory.

"Tell me about your girl, the one who went into England," Cat invited.

"Wenna? I haven't seen her for close on thirty years. She must be nearly fifty now."

"Why did she go into England?"

"She was married young and widowed young when her man was killed in the quarry. She wanted a new life."

"And married a Falcon cousin," Cat prompted.

"Many years later and he was much younger than she. They have a farm now and a son called Giles."

"Are they very rich?" Cat took another gulp of tea.

"I suppose so. I never thought about it."

"And they must all live in a grand, big house. The Falcons, I mean. Do you think they have a motor-car?"

"I suppose so. I really couldn't say."

"If we went into England we'd have to go on a train, wouldn't we?" Cat said eagerly.

"I've never been on a train in my life," the old woman said firmly, "and at my age I'm not starting now. Shall I tell you the story of Gelert and how his master thought he'd eaten the baby? You always did like that one."

"Yes. That's a good story," Cat leaned back against the pillow and folded her hands together. She had heard the tale many times, or rather the beginning of it, for Aunt Catrin usually nodded off to sleep long before the end was reached.

"There was once a great prince who lived on the island of Anglesey . . ."

The old voice, strongly accented, droned on. Cat's eyes fixed upon the darkening panes of glass, dreamed of rich Falcons and a big house called Kingsmead.

Chapter 2

Michael Shaw had been working all day and was weary to the bone. He had come out at his own expense, the War Office refusing to finance a war artist in his mid-seventies. Not that he looked or felt his age. There was not an ounce of spare flesh on his wiry frame, and his thick curly hair retained much of its original blackness.

He sat now in a canvas chair at the end of the long wooden hut and doodled idly on the sketch pad he carried. Tiny faces, some with open, screaming mouths, others with eyes narrowed against gunsmoke, filled the page. All around him was the ceaseless bustle of a field hospital. Doctors, gray with fatigue, hurried past mattresses piled with blood-soaked, sweating wounded. The stench of urine and vomit, the sounds of moaning and cursing, the rasp of saw against amputated bone, the scarlet and russet of gaping wounds in mud-encrusted flesh—he had depicted them over and over in the six months since he had come to France.

His hands, moving of their own volition without the conscious direction of his brain, drew another face upon the crowded page. A round girlish face with a tail of hair over one shoulder and large eyes that gazed out dreamily above a down-slanting smile.

He looked down in slight surprise at what he had drawn. Even here, in this place of maimed and dying, Beth Falcon stole in memory. Not a night passed that she did not hover at the edge of his dreams. Not a morning dawned that he did not open his eyes in the hope that she might be standing there.

He had known her for one summer more than a quarter of a century before. He had been on a sketching holiday and had lodged on the Falcon estate. In his mind that summer had been all gold and silver, with Beth in her green dress and ridiculous straw hat. She had been eighteen, too young for him, too eager to love, too ready to give. It had been easy for him to take, incredibly hard for him to leave when the summer was over and return to a nagging wife for whom he felt nothing but a dutiful pity.

He had not known she was expecting his child, had heard only that she was dead, at the very time that his wife had died and he would have been free to offer marriage. The tragedy had almost destroyed him for a long time, but out of it had come a compulsion to paint so strong that he had resigned his safe occupation and over the years established himself as a talented artist with a small but exclusive following.

Nine years before he had learned for the first time of the existence of his daughter. She had paid him one brief visit at his studio and gone away again, having apparently satisfied her curiosity. Her name had been Levanah. An odd name, but she had been an odd young woman, her eyes yellow as a fox's, her hair a clear light red hanging straight and thick below her ears. There had been nothing in her of Beth's sweetness, and yet when she had left he had been strongly tempted to go after her.

Since then he had heard nothing of her, though from time to time vague word of the Falcons had reached his ears. He believed she had married one of them, but had not troubled to inquire further. He had felt no fatherly instinct toward the yellow-eyed girl, only a profound pity that Beth should have died and their happiness been so fugitive a thing.

He yawned, weariness shackling his limbs. In a few minutes he would get up and go in search of a cup of tea. Meanwhile he let his eyelids droop, the sounds about him muting, he remembered scents of other days drowning the stench of the ward.

"Mr. Shaw, there's tea brewed at the end of the ward." A medical orderly, fresh-faced and deferential, tapped his shoulder.

"I'll get some. Thanks."

He smiled back at the ingenuous face, thinking, *God! they get younger!*, and made his way down the narrow alley between the mattresses. Outside the hut the wind was rising, churning the mud. One of the surgeons cursed as the hurricane lamp above his head swung in a sudden draft.

Michael stopped, his attention caught by a young man who lay on a rough stretcher near the wall. Still short of thirty, with sweat-darkened fair hair, the man had the pinched, yellow look of the dying. A blanket, red-sodden, covered him but his fingers plucked ceaselessly at its hem.

"Would you like some tea?"

The older man knelt, aware of something familiar in the pain-wracked features. The blue eyes regarded him with a kind of dull curiosity, as if the boy were puzzled by his own condition.

"Some tea?" Michael asked again.

The dying man moved his head in a negative way. His lips, cracked and swollen, shaped a word but only a sigh emerged.

Michael, forgetting his own thirst, leaned closer. The blue eyes had the clear, blank look of surprise generally associated with the newborn except that the newborn, from the little Michael had seen of them, came into the world with secret knowledge in their faces.

His hands moved, turning the sketch pad to a blank page, gripping the pencil more securely. Deeper than his pity was the desire to capture that blank innocence of dying. He was no longer weary. The lust to create rose up in him like sexual passion. In one part of himself he loved the young man for dying.

"Levanah," said the young man so clearly that, for a moment, Michael was not sure who had spoken. The word came again, more strongly.

"Levanah."

"What of her?" Michael lifted his pencil from the paper, frowning. His daughter was named Levanah. It was not a common name. And the young man's face was familiar, like a face he had known many years before.

"Tell her Teddy died. He was helping me. Tell Wenna—"

"Who is Wenna?"

"Wife. My wife." The words came raspingly now.

"Tell her what? What shall I tell her?"

"Evil. Levanah—the smell of evil. Help Wenna." The fingers clutching at the blanket were still.

"You are—?" Michael asked the question urgently, afraid that it was too late.

But the blue eyes were still aware, the cracked lips still moving.

"Cal Falcon," said the gasping voice. "Teddy and I—" The last words lifted in surprise, the eyes shifting beyond Michael and staring there with no flicker of pupil or lash.

"Cal Falcon," Michael said. It was as good an epitaph as any.

The eyes were dulling rapidly, the surprise blurring into acceptance.

His hands began to move again, the pencil strokes black in the fading light. In the motionless figure on the stretcher there was a kind of triumph.

Somebody came up and bent to close the eyes, to pull the rough blanket over the face. A fresh batch of wounded had arrived and were being hustled in, some of them walking, others being unloaded from the horse-drawn ambulances. The space would soon be needed.

The rough drawing was almost complete. He would finish it later, but the spirit of the original impulse was already embodied in the lines and spaces and etched blocks of scribbled lead.

He had no interest in drinking tea. There was a village near, out of bounds to the military, but there was still an inn there which he patronized on the rare occasions when he craved alcohol.

As he walked away from the sandbagged area down the rutted lane he felt a lifting of depression. Pain and death no longer horrified him, but they wound a miasma of hopelessness about him. The men were so young and they died with what seemed to him appalling ease. Yet he, older than any of them, survived. It was, he sometimes thought, as if their dying nourished his own talents.

But he was pleased with his day's work. When he went back to England he would hold an exhibition of his drawings. He would make people understand the ugly reality of the war they read about so complacently over their breakfast tables. Perhaps if a sufficient number of people could be made to understand there would be an end to the hating. If that happened he would be able to justify his own survival.

The village had been a prosperous community once. Now with battle advancing like an inexorable tide and the crops trampled down by marching boots, many of the inhabitants had fled. He had seen them leaving other villages, the old women in rusty black with patient, bewildered faces sitting on top of piles of bedding, pots and pans, the children leading broken-down ponies whose ribs showed pitifully as they tugged along the laden carts, the old men spitting streams of tobacco juice into the ditches. Straggling lines of human beings moving aimlessly through a bullet-scarred landscape.

Grass grew up now between the cobbles and most of the glass in the windows had been broken. The men and boys had long since gone. So had many of the women, but a few still remained, clinging obstinately to their homes, trying to pretend that what was happening was no more than a bad dream and that, one day, the soldiers would leave and everything would be as it had been before.

Yvonne was sitting at the usual table when he walked in. She was hunched over a glass of pernod, her broad face intent on the milky liquid as she stirred it round with a long-handled spoon.

Michael watched her from the shadow of the doorway. There was at that moment a soothing tranquillity about her thickset figure and the wing of brown hair that fell across her cheek. The tranquillity was an illusion, of course. Yvonne had a restless, sullen nature that craved constant gaiety. She had told him once that she was married, but he suspected that her husband was invented, as was the château in which she declared she had spent her childhood.

She had sensed his presence and looked up from her drink, pushing back her hair with a coy, self-conscious gesture that destroyed what fleeting attractions she possessed. Her voice, quick and hovering perpetually on the edge of shrillness, rose into the silence of the dusty bar.

"So you come to seek my company, old friend? Will you drink with me? This is the last bottle, I fear."

He answered her in her own tongue, long periods in France having accustomed him to the language.

"It was a long day and I'm tired."

"Too tired?" she asked, flouncing broad hips as she rose to get another glass.

"Not too tired," he said, taking the seat she had just vacated. The chair was still warm, and as she took her place opposite him he was stirred by the heaviness of her breasts under the cheap blouse.

"You English are all the same," she said, pouting. "Women and women and more women."

"In England we have similar notions about the French," he said dryly.

"Let us drink to the mingling of—ideas then." She raised her glass and smiled at him. It was a practiced

smile that stripped her of the last vestiges of innocence. Raising his own glass he thought that it was
better so. In this world the innocent did not survive.

"I heard much shooting today," she said, clinking
her glass to his. "On my way back from confession I
heard the shooting. Were many killed?"

"Many," he said somberly, "and one of them—I
knew his family. It was strange, watching him die.
He left a wife. She won't know yet that she's a
widow."

"Perhaps I too am a widow," Yvonne said dole-
fully. "It is many months since I saw him or heard
from him. Perhaps I too am a widow."

"You'll survive," Michael said.

"But of course." She shrugged plump shoulders. "I
will be here long after the war is ended. Here, in my
little bar, with the customers coming back."

"And your husband probably," he said cheerfully.

"Oh, him too." She took another mouthful of pernod and said, "Without him I am desolate."

"Yes, of course."

"You must not blame me that I seek consolation,"
she said testily. "A poor woman, who might be a
widow, has the right to seek a little comfort. And
you are glad of a warm bed on cold nights."

"Very glad."

"And the hour grows late." She slanted him a
glance. "There are onions here but no meat. I could
make a stew if you like."

"I'm not hungry."

"Then we'll go to bed." She rose without haste and
went ahead of him up the wooden stairs. Seen from
below her figure had the odd, foreshortened aspect of
a doll cut out of cardboard. There was an unreality

about her, and in a sudden, almost childish panic he hurried after her.

Her bedroom had the same undusted air as the bar. Without being either dirty or untidy the room gave off an impression of sluttishness held in check by only the remnants of housewifely pride. A large crucifix draped with a rosary hung on the wall, the only other ornament being a big doll with red satin skirts who perched near the head of the bed. A sailor had brought it for her from Paris, she had told him once. It simpered at him now, despising him.

His own clothes shed, he lay in bed, stretching into the warmth. It would have been pleasant to sleep, to lose himself in oblivion, but Yvonne was taking off her clothes in the slow coy manner that had amused him when he had first known her, but now it irritated him. Her thighs were too slack, her stomach too bulging, and when she joined him the faint, stale smell of unwashed flesh rose to his nostrils.

But she was warm and waiting and the hunger for life still filled him unappeased. He took her speedily, closing his eyes, trying not to hear her dutiful little moans. Sometimes it crossed his mind that she cared as little for sexual pleasure as his wife had done, but Susan had pushed him away long before he was satisfied while Yvonne played the part expected of her, wriggling and panting as mechanically as a puppet.

"You have the vigor of a much younger man," she said. It was true, but as she said the same thing on every occasion, the compliment had lost its savor.

"Did I please you?"

She always asked that question too. He put his arm round her and said kindly, "You always please me."

"But not as much as the other girl."

"What other girl?"

"The one whose name you spoke so often in your sleep. The one named Beth."

His arm stiffened under her neck and she rolled away, propping her chin on her hands.

"This Beth," she persisted. "Tell me of her. Was she beautiful?"

He shook his head, speaking slowly in an effort to draw her into his own thoughts.

"She was rain and sunshine," he said. "One following the other like April. She was small and young with the bloom on her like a peach. But she was not beautiful though you would not have guessed it until you looked at her closely."

"Did she die?" Yvonne asked.

"She died," he said.

"When she was still young?"

"At nineteen." His voice, in the lamplit room, had the harshness of a too well remembered pain. "She bore a child and then she killed herself."

"Your child?"

"My daughter. I knew nothing of it until years afterward when I met my daughter for the first and only time. Before that I knew only that Beth had died."

"And the child? You only saw her once!"

"Only once. She was a strange girl."

Into his mind had come a picture of Levanah when she had called to see him at his London studio. She had been small like Beth, with her mother's honey hair darkened to red, but there had been nothing in her of Beth's vulnerable sweetness. Levanah had been all sharp angles, and narrow yellow eyes, and hands that clenched upon the brim of her straw hat as if it were a weapon. Yet when she had gone he had fought down the impulse to follow her, to warn her—of what he had no idea.

"This Beth," Yvonne said. "If she had lived you would not have loved her so much. You are like many men. You love dreams, and memories."

"Perhaps." He thought reluctantly that it was true. He lived much of his life in a dream, translating reality into painted canvas and penciled sketch pad.

"I am a real woman," Yvonne said. "You use me as you please, and in your sleep cry out the name of a dead girl."

"You've done well enough out of me too," he said shortly, and thought of the money he left on the dresser after every visit he made.

"I shall go to confession tomorrow," Yvonne said virtuously.

He grinned, aware that she used the confessional rather as another woman might use a laxative, to purge herself after a feast so that she could indulge in more gluttony.

"It is not comic!" she said indignantly. "You do not know how I suffer, to have to live as I do. The world is cruel to women."

"Cruel to us all," he agreed, and wished he felt something more than a kind of contemptuous gratitude for her.

"If my husband is still alive he must often think of me," she said complacently. "It must fret his mind not to know what I am doing. He was a most jealous man, most jealous."

She gave a hopeful, sideways look, but Michael allowed himself to yawn. It mattered nothing to him whether Yvonne's husband, if she had one, were jealous or not. It occurred to him just before he fell asleep that very little really mattered to him at all.

Even death had become meaningless, no more than lead marks on a paper and the blurred gaze of a man who reminded him of Beth.

It was new-washed dawn when he woke and Yvonne was still asleep and snoring. As he dressed he was reminded of that other departure he had made. Not from a dusty inn, but from the small house on Falcon land, he had ridden away. Beth had been awake, still warm from loving, and it had taken all his self-control to leave her without turning back. Her face had been flushed and her hair untidy, gleams of sunlight edging the tousled strands. He had known that every part of her cried out to hold him back, but she had left the words unspoken. In the end she had lacked the courage to make demands, and he had never seen her again except in dreams and in the look of a dying man's face.

He left money on the dresser, gave Yvonne a look in which there was no desire, and emerged into the grass-grown street.

The air smelled of rotting flesh and cordite. Across the fields puffs of gunsmoke drifted up into the morning sky. Many of the houses along the street had been scored by shrapnel, their facades like the faces of wounded men. A thin cat danced across the road, its tail high, its paws dainty as the feet of a ballerina. Michael watched it with vague uneasiness rising up in him. He was not sure at first why the animal should arouse such a feeling in him. Then he remembered that Levanah, his daughter, had moved in the same way and her eyes had been yellow and hungry too.

"Poor little thing!" a voice said at Michael's elbow. "Many of them have been eaten. Food is difficult to obtain."

"Good morning, Father." Michael shook hands with the small curé whose eyes peered up at him from under a thatch of graying hair. The curé was about ten years the artist's junior but looked older, his shoulders hunched as if they bore the weight of too many confessions.

"You have been—visiting?"

The faint reproof in the other's voice stamped him as a man of the cloth. His imperceptible shrug marked him as a Frenchman.

"It is good to find shelter in these times," Michael said evasively.

"The fighting was bad yesterday," the priest said. "The shelling and the gunfire. Many died. This was a peaceful village once, but now the world has gone mad."

"It always was," Michael said somberly.

The two men stood silently, their eyes fixed upon the cat, who, having chosen a patch of pale sunlight, lay down in it, stretching luxuriously. Its tongue flicked out at them mockingly.

"I must make ready to offer Mass," the priest said at last. He glanced, without much hope, at his companion. "No doubt I will be needed afterward in the confessional." This time his shrug was definitely Gallic.

"Good day to you, Father." Michael shook his hand cordially.

As he plodded, wheezing a little, toward the church, Michael was reminded of his wife. Odd that he should not have thought of Susan for twenty years, and now he saw her clearly, plump and discontented, stopping at the bend in the staircase to puff and pant and complain that he had forgotten to do something or other.

The priest, still wheezing, disappeared within the shadow of the porch. The cat had leapt away and over to the south the guns started firing again.

He was weary of it all, weary of the slaughter and the ravaged landscape and the unlovely woman whom he paid in order to be assured that he was still alive. He was weary of the memories that tormented him; Beth who had died and so cheated them both; Levanah who had visited him briefly and walked away; and now the picture of Susan whom he had never been able to admit he hated.

Thinking of her now he knew that his hatred, once acknowledged, had died. He no longer felt anything for the woman to whom he had been married, beyond a vague wonder that he had endured her nagging for so long.

Beth and Levanah remained. Their ghosts, for in his mind his daughter was as dead as his lover, had to be exorcised. But not here, not in this war-torn place. He would go home again. And to Michael Shaw home had become, not his London studio, but the village where he had spent one summer of his life.

Marie Regina, with its cobbled street, and the wooden bridge under which the river flowed, or rushed according to the season, came into his thoughts, and he longed for it as if he were longing for a woman.

Chapter 3

He had traveled by train from London and taken a cab to the village, for though Marie Regina lay on the direct route between London and Maidstone, Falcon influence had curved the railway line to the southeast avoiding the thickly wooded estate of Kingsmead and the hamlet itself, preserving unspoiled the wheat-cool meadows and proud hop fields and the ruins of the old monastery that rose on the hill beyond the river. Not quite unspoiled, he thought, noticing that the old wooden bridge had been replaced by a stone edifice. But the street that sloped down from the main highway into the village was as he remembered it, and the village itself had not changed. Its houses still huddled together down the winding street and spread out around the green with its pond and the tall Maypole against which successive generations of ministers had fulminated in vain.

He booked a room at the inn, remembering how, on that other occasion, he had ridden horseback down the highway and, before he had reached the village, a girl had glided out into the darkness.

It had been his first meeting with Beth Falcon
and not until the next day had he seen her face. She
had been a shape and a voice in the darkness, and not
until later did he realize that he had paused to listen
to a mating call.

The landlady at the inn was a stranger. He
presumed the people who owned it twenty years before had sold up and moved away. From the window
of his room he could look out across the green to the
church with its tall spire and the graveyard that
sloped up behind it to the level ground beyond. Generations of villagers were buried there and the largest
tomb belonged to the Falcons. Beth had shown it to
him, tracing the golden names with her forefinger,
squinting into the sunshine.

"The last one laid here was Willow Falcon. She
was killed by the falling of a tree and as she lay dying she said, 'Victory will not come until a falcon
rides upon a moth.' Wasn't that a strange thing to
say! But then she was one of the witch women and
bore the mark."

Beth had borne the mark herself; a crescent moon
etched in purple on her thigh, and there were times
when her eyes became as blank as water and she
spoke of things she could not have known. But her
own end had been shielded from her, and there had
been only loving in her witchcraft.

"The meal is not up to much," the landlady apologized as she served it. "Most of the menfolk are away
at the war and the place is quiet at this end of the
year. Indeed you're the only guest, sir."

He assured her, truthfully, that the meal was excellent, and inquired if there had been many casualties
in the neighborhood.

"No more than half a dozen, sir, and none of them

my own family," she said. "Young Lord Falcon was killed some months back. Lord Edward that was, though most folk called him Teddy. Very free and easy in his ways, sir. Friendly with everybody. He and his cousin, Caleb Falcon, were killed on the same day."

"The Falcons live here, do they?"

"Over at Kingsmead, sir. The big estate on the left as you drive toward the bridge. The land on the other side of the river is Falcon land too. Miss Leah had a school built there, and most of the children hereabouts attend it, until they're big enough to go to Maidstone County. But most of them leave off schooling at fourteen and work on the land, though some drift to the big cities now where the wages are higher."

"Times are changing," Michael said.

"Indeed they are, sir!" The landlady beamed as if he had said something of startling originality. "Why, in the five years since my late husband and I bought this place, we've seen Marie Regina alter. There were three shops when we came here and now there are six, if you please. And an omnibus goes twice a week to Maidstone. And it's not just places that change, sir. Time was when a girl was proud to go into service for her board and keep and a shilling a week all found. Now they want half a crown and two days off a month, if you please. And they're not as respectful as they might be. Setting themselves up as good as the gentry, they are!"

"But the old ways still persist in some places." Michael drank the coffee cautiously and found it more palatable than he had expected.

"The Falcons are still bred to the old ways," she said. "For all his free and easy ways, Lord Teddy was a gentleman. One had only to look at him to see that. Cal Falcon had the same air for all that he was born on the wrong side of the blanket."

"Oh?"

The landlady struggled for a moment between the desire to sit and gossip and the conviction that she ought to be getting on with some work. Desire won and she sat down on a chair near the table.

"They're an old family, you see," she said. "They do say there have been Falcons here since the time of Henry the Eighth, living up at the big house, increasing their land through marriage and the Lord knows how else. My late husband and I come from the other side of Maidstone, and at one time the Falcons owned a house there too. Paget Place it was called. Lord Teddy sold it, and bought some racehorses, but I don't think they ever won anything important."

"And Cal Falcon?" He tried gently to lead her back to the original subject.

Proving less troublesome than the racehorses, she obliged with, "He was Miss Edith's son. There were five of them at one time, sir. Miss Leah, Miss Edith, Lord John and Miss Beth. Oh, and another brother but he emigrated and I can't think of his name. Lord John was killed in a riding accident and left a son—that was Teddy. Miss Leah was a widow with a little girl of her own. Miss Edith and Miss Beth— they both had children too, though neither of them was wed. Miss Beth killed herself, poor soul, after her daughter was born. Miss Leah brought the girl up with her own child and Teddy. Miss Edith moved to Whittle Farm over the other side of the hill, and reared Cal herself. She's dead now and Cal too."

"Did he marry?"

"He wed his cousin, sir. Wenna Davies her name was, and she was years older than him, a widow for ages when she married him. From Wales she came. There's always been Welsh blood in the family."

"And Teddy? Did he marry?"

"He wed his cousin, Levanah," the landlady said. "Miss Beth's love child, that is."

"And so there are two Falcon widows."

"Three. Miss Leah still lives up at Kingsmead."

"And Miss—er—Levanah?"

"Lady Falcon? She lives at Kingsmead too." An indefinable air of reserve had crept into the landlady's face.

"It must be lonely," he persisted.

"There are two children," the landlady said. "Twins—a boy and a girl. Johnny and Selena."

Michael wondered what would happen if he said to her, "They are my grandchildren. I am the lover over whom Beth Falcon killed herself."

"But they're a fine family," the landlady was saying. "An old family with tradition behind them, and now two of their young men gone. I used to regret that I'd never had children, but not now. You're lucky not to be of an age to be in the war yourself, sir."

"Yes, indeed."

"Will you be wanting anything else?" she inquired.

"Thank you, no. I've eaten too much already."

"There isn't very much to do here in the evenings, sir," she said doubtfully, as if she suspected him of craving wild gaieties.

"I shall take a walk," he told her, and submitted to being helped on with his overcoat.

The evening was drawing in, the sky glowing

through lemon to deepest orange, the sun muting itself below the horizon, the trees rustling in a breeze
that spiraled up from the tall grasses.

He had brought no drawing materials with him
and, for an instant, felt a pang of regret. His career
had become his whole life, and there were times
when he felt himself to be a prisoner of his own tal-
ent. The days when he could enjoy beauty for its
own sake without wanting to express it had long
since gone.

He crossed the road and went through the gate
into the churchyard. A path meandered between the
moss-grown graves to the brow of the hill. He
walked slowly, proud of the fact that he needed no
stick, that his bearing was still erect, his hair only
slightly receding.

The Falcon tomb, with its sword-bearing stone angel guarding the triple-locked door, dominated part
of the ground. He paused briefly, reading the names,
threw an indifferent glance toward the newer graves
and went on up to the low wall that divided the cem-
etery from the meadow beyond.

Beth, as a suicide, was buried beyond the wall. He
had passed through Marie Regina once since her
death, and had spent a few minutes of bitter regret
before riding on. He scaled the low parapet without
appreciable difficulty and found the grave, its headstone bleakly inscribed,

ELIZABETH FALCON
Born 1870. Died 1889

The grass around the plot had been neatly clipped
and a bunch of fading flowers drooped over the sides
of a stone jug. He stared at it for a long time,

remembering with unbearable charity how she had stood almost on the very spot, her April face wistful as she told the tale of another girl buried in that same meadow.

"She was a girl from Wales who married a Falcon long ago. She bore the devil's kiss and was swum as a witch by the villagers. They believed in those days that if an accused witch floated she was guilty. Catrin Falcon drowned, which meant she was innocent, but they buried her outside the churchyard just to be safe."

She had laughed at the end of the tale, but there had been tears in her eyes too and she had parted the grass about the sunken headstone with tender fingers.

Michael moved away from the grave, pain stabbing behind his own eyes. He decided irritably that he needed spectacles, for the scene before him blurred and shook. His legs ached and he sat down on the wall, resting his head in his hands, wishing he had never come.

A rustle attracted his attention, followed by the clink of stone on stone. He raised his head and saw that a woman was putting fresh flowers into the vase.

It was Beth twenty-seven years on, her thick hair swinging in its tail down her back, her hands curved around the stems of the blossoms. He watched her with breathless delight as the long mourning fell away, and it was summer again.

Then she turned and started toward him and it was not Beth, though the features were similar. But this woman was past middle age, her hair streaked with white, her eyes narrower than Beth's had been and, even in the fading light, brilliantly green. She was dressed simply in a black gown with a shawl of some green material knotted about her shoulders.

"Good evening." She stopped in front of him, nodding pleasantly, but with a question in her voice.

"Good evening. It's a warm day," he said, feeling his way back cautiously to reality.

"For the time of year." She gave him a lopsided grin that reminded him of Beth so vividly that he exclaimed, "But you must be Cousin Wenna!"

"I am Wenna Falcon," she said, puzzlement increasing in her face. "Have we met before?"

"I've seen you, many years ago when you were teaching at the school here," he said. "That was before your marriage when Beth was alive."

She frowned, peering at him closely as if something in him awakened her own recollection.

"You are the artist to whom Beth rented the cottage!" she exclaimed.

"Michael Shaw," he said, nodding.

Wenna sat down abruptly on the wall next to him and gave a long, low whistle. The unexpectedly boyish reaction broke the tension and he found himself laughing. It had been years since he had laughed, and it seemed, not irreverent, but natural and right that he should be amused in this place near to Beth's grave.

"After all this time!" Wenna exclaimed. "But you can't know—"

"That Beth had a daughter? I didn't know anything of it until a few years ago when Levanah came to see me at my studio in London. She had tracked me down in a manner of speaking, but I saw her only the one time. When I went back to my wife I didn't know Beth was carrying my child. Her sister let me know that she had died, but even then she didn't mention there was a child."

"That sounds like Leah," Wenna said. "She took care of Levanah as if she'd been her own."

"Mary?"

Wenna nodded and pressed her lips together before she spoke again.

"Leah was always too possessive," she said slowly. "Both Mary and Levanah rebelled against it. Levanah went to stay in London for a time and then she spent a year in Wales with my mother. When she came back she married Teddy."

"And her own daughter?"

"Mary? She left home with an assistant teacher who was employed at the school. An odd, mannish young woman called Charlotte Bishop. We've heard nothing of either of them for years."

"And you married a Falcon."

She nodded, humor creasing the corners of her eyes and lips.

"Does it shock you?" she inquired. "I was forty when I married Edith Falcon's son and he was not twenty. Funny to think I'd been a widow for as long as he'd been alive. My first husband was killed in the quarry when we'd been wed only three months. That was why I left Wales and came to Kingsmead in the first place. And I've never gone back."

"And you wed Edith's son."

"Edith had just died and Cal was alone at Whittle Farm," she said. "We suited each other, and we were happy. He was very proud of our son. Giles is eight now. Eight years old."

"I understand you're a widow again," he said delicately.

"Three months ago," she said. "He and Teddy Falcon were killed on the same day, on the Somme. We heard they were killed outright. I hope it was true."

He said nothing, remembering the smell of blood and urine in the field hospital, remembering the pain-wracked face of the fair-haired young man who had whispered, "Evil. Levanah—the smell of evil. Help Wenna."

"So we are both widows, your daughter and I," she said.

With a little shock of surprise he realized it was true. It was hard to picture the thin, hungry-eyed girl who had visited his studio as a settled matron in black.

"And she had children!" Wenna exclaimed. "Twins. Johnny and Selena are six years old. You have grandchildren, Mr. Shaw."

"Michael, please, otherwise I shall feel older than I am," he protested.

"Michael then, and you must call me Wenna," she said promptly.

"Thank you." He held out his hand and she shook it warmly.

Her own palm was slightly roughened to the touch, her cuticles ragged. She intercepted his glance and said lightly, "When I heard Cal was dead I had such an ache in my heart that I set to work in the garden to ease it a little. Lord! but I practically wore out the soil with digging and hoeing! But when the darkness came and I couldn't see to work outdoors then I sat by the fire and pulled at my fingers. Pulled off bits of skin until the tips of my fingers were raw. Such silly things women do when they are grieved!"

He was inexpressibly touched by her words, so much so that he reached out and took her hand again.

"You are still at the farm?" he asked.

"With Giles," she answered, nodding. "He's a fine boy, like his father in looks and temperament."

"It must be lonely for you," he said.

"Better be lonely than up at the big house," Wenna said.

"At Kingsmead? Why?"

"It's a gloomy place," she said evasively. "The farm is more cheerful, even with Cal gone. But tell me about yourself. I guessed years ago who Levanah's father was, but she never spoke of it and I'd no idea she'd ever met you. But you were the only man with whom Beth ever spent any time alone. And I've seen your name since in art reviews. You're a famous man now."

"Well-known in a particular field," he corrected modestly.

"And you spend a lot of your time abroad. I read that somewhere too."

"I came back from France a month ago."

"France!" She looked at him in surprise. "You were out there?"

"Greatly to the annoyance of several military gentlemen who thought I was far too ancient to be allowed out of my wheelchair," he said.

"You look very young," she said. "Very distinguished, if I may say so."

"Like an old piece of furniture," he joked.

"And after all this time," she marveled, "you've come back to Marie Regina! Beth's lover returned."

"Thirty years too late," he said.

"Things happen. It's easy to look back and blame ourselves," she said. "Beth was always a strange, fanciful creature. I used to wonder sometimes what would become of her. She had not the courage to go on living without hope."

Looking at Wenna, Michael thought that she

would always find the courage to go on living. There was both strength and dignity in the quiet face with its humorous mouth and sleepy, thick-lashed green eyes. The white bands in her brown hair were like moonlight.

"You look very young yourself," he said impulsively.

"I am almost fifty. Like yourself, I'm well preserved," she countered, but a faint pinkness had crept into her cheeks and her glance was shy. A moment later she asked, "Are you here to see Levanah? Have you been to Kingsmead?"

"I'm staying in the village," he told her. "Levanah hasn't seen me for years, and she doesn't know I'm here now."

"Would you like to walk back to the farm and have some supper with me?" she asked. "Or were you thinking of going to Kingsmead at once?"

"In a day or two. It would be unfair to intrude on her grief without warning."

"Grief?" For an instant her smile had a downward twist. Then she rose, pulling her shawl into place. "The farm is just over the bridge, at the other side of the hill."

"I remember it." He also rose and smiled at her. "I'd like to see Giles, if he's still awake."

"He'll be awake. Giles is a night bird like me."

"And you came up here to put flowers."

"Somebody has to respect her memory," she said simply. "I meant to bring a jug of fresh water but I forgot. My memory is not what it was since I gave up schoolteaching!"

"And mine was never any good at all," he said ruefully. "Someone came in the other day and asked if

Mr. Shaw was in, and I found myself getting up and offering to look for him."

She threw back her head and laughed delightedly. She had a beautiful laugh, warm and rich, the muscles of her sunbrowned throat working.

His wife Susan had seldom laughed save in a prim, pained way as if she feared there might be some offense in it. Beth's laughter had floated out of her, wild as a birdsong. Wenna laughed with her eyes as well as her throat, the skin crinkling deeply, her plain face flowering into a rare beauty.

With great pleasure he was aware that the sound still had power to stir him to desire.

The rest had refreshed him, and he enjoyed the walk across the field and down the main road to the bridge. Beyond the bridge, on the right, the ruins of the ancient monastery brooded against the darkening sky.

Whittle Farm was at the far side of the hill. It was hidden from the road by a high wall, its fields arched about it.

"Did Beth ever tell you that the farm has been part of the Falcon estate since the eighteenth century?" Wenna asked, opening the gate. "When Edith Falcon got herself into trouble her brother John was still alive. He gave her the farm, much to Leah's displeasure, and Cal was born here."

The house was not large but it was warm and clean, not with the aggressive cleanliness of a house scrubbed by an unloved woman, but with a mellow, welcoming glow. There were books piled on shelves against the walls, red and orange leaves flaming in a copper bowl, a half-finished tapestry in its frame.

"The girls sleep in the village," Wenna said, leading the way into a large bright kitchen where, amid the comfortable clutter, a small boy sat at a long table fitting together a model train. As the others came in he slid to his feet and gave a neat, old-fashioned bow. He was a good-looking child, tall for his age with a cowlick of straight blond hair and eyes as green as his mother's.

"Giles, Michael Shaw is—an old friend of the family," Wenna said.

"How do you do, Giles?" Michael shook hands gravely.

"I'll make some tea," said Wenna.

"Would you like to help me with my train?" Giles asked politely. "The wheels won't go round properly."

"I'm not very mechanically minded, I'm afraid," Michael apologized, allowing himself to be taken captive by a small, grubby hand.

Wenna was removing her shawl, poking the fire into a blaze. The warmth of the room became a living, tangible quality. Michael felt himself relaxing into it, the tensions of the long years dissolving.

"You're making a terrible mess of it," Giles said critically. "My daddy could mend anything, but he's had to go and be dead."

"Giles remembers him," Wenna said, "though it's two years since he went."

"It's right that he should," Michael said. "Your daddy was a very brave man, Giles."

"He could mend things too," said Giles.

"But Mr. Shaw can paint pictures," Wenna declared, setting out cups. "If you ask him nicely he may paint one for you one day."

"Yes. Of course I will." He gave Wenna a smile over the bent fair head and saw her answering smile beam out into the room.

Chapter 4

Levanah Falcon stood before the long mirror in her dressing room and examined her reflection critically. She had lost a little weight since news of Teddy's death had been brought to her, and in the black gown she had a hungry air. Under the narrowly slanting eyes her cheekbones stood out sharply. Her hair caught back in the nape of her neck with a black ribbon was a clear, light red. On the forefinger of her left hand a black pearl gleamed dully.

Black, she decided, suited her pale complexion and gave an air of restrained mystery to her appearance. She was twenty-seven years old but might, with her strangely enigmatic expression and unusual coloring, have been any age.

Satisfied, she turned from the glass and cast a long, sweeping look about the dressing room and through the half-open door into the bedroom beyond. These two rooms were in the original Tudor part of Kingsmead, built over the solar and parlor. The carved oak panels of the walls, the tester bed with its

49

embroidered hangings took one back into a richer
and more colorful age.

She was still thinking about herself as she walked
along the portrait-lined gallery to the wide stone
staircase that led down to the great hall. The hall
with its few pieces of time-blackened furniture, its
faded tapestries, its array of silver and gilt dishes,
stretched up to the hammer-beam roof. The vast
apartment had been the scene of many dramatic
events in the centuries since the first Sir Harry Falcon had built it on land granted to him as a reward
for his part in despoiling the local monastery. It was
here that two Falcon brothers had pledged allegiance
to different sides during the Civil War. On the
stairs Regina Falcon, the Stuart king's mistress, had
waited for news of her little, lame daughter Prayer;
and a later Falcon daughter, cheated of her love, had
slashed her cheek with a knife. It was into this hall
that the villagers had carried her Uncle John, killed
like his father before him in a fall from his horse,
and the following week her own mother, having
borne her bastard and killed herself in lonely despair,
had been carried out to the waiting hearse.

Levanah's red lips curved into the shape of a smile.
Beth Falcon had been a weak fool for all her gazing
into a crystal ball and the witch mark on her leg. She
had allowed herself to be defeated by her own loving
nature. Levanah, brought up in the great house with
her cousins, Teddy and Mary, had twisted life to her
own design. She had married Teddy and borne him
twins, and been a good wife. And Teddy had been
obliging enough to die, along with her bastard
cousin, Cal. The thought of them both dying together had pleased her sense of what was fitting. During her girlhood Cal had been ready to fall in love

with her for a time, but in the end he had married Cousin Wenna, who was years older than he was and plain into the bargain. Levanah had never really forgiven him for that. It was right that Wenna should be left a widow too.

On the wall behind her portraits of the successive owners of Kingsmead and their wives hung against the stone wall. The original manor, the great hall acting as general living area, had consisted of four rooms downstairs and four bedchambers above. Late owners had added the two wings that stretched out at right angles to the main block, thus forming a capital *E* with the middle stroke missing. The twins had their rooms over the kitchen quarters in one wing. The large sitting room over the drawing room in the other wing had been converted into a nursery for them. She had been giving them lessons in reading and writing for nearly a year, but both had been entered at expensive boarding schools and would start the following year.

As she thought of money her smooth brow creased slightly. Falcon land spread its thousand acres on both sides of the river, but the war had brought changes. Most of the laboring men had either volunteered or been conscripted into the army, and much of the previous season's crop had gone to seed for lack of harvesters. Food prices were rising steeply, as was the price of everything else. And Teddy had not been clever with money. An expensive and unprofitable string of horses, a disastrous flutter in a diamond mine that had proved to be non-existent, a luxury yacht which he had been forced to sell at a loss—all these had made deep inroads into the family fortune. All things considered it was as well that he had been killed. As her son's guardian Levanah now held the purse strings and she was determined that neither Johnny nor Selena would ever want for anything.

A movement behind her broke into her musing. Aunt Leah had come out of the nursery and was standing watching her. Like her niece she wore black and her chignon of gray hair was hidden under a black veil. Her eyes, fixed on Levanah, were bright.

"You really hate me, don't you?" Levanah said softly, meeting their gaze. "You would like to push me down these stairs to the stone below, wouldn't you, Aunt dear? Why don't you then? Why don't you try?"

"The children are not in their room," Leah said.

"They went into the village with Jane to buy some sweets. Are you coming down for coffee, Aunt? It's close on eleven."

"I had some tea earlier."

"But you'll bear me company while I drink mine? We can talk about Teddy if you wish. Poor Teddy to die so young! Do you believe that he was killed outright? I think they say that to all the relatives to spare their feelings, don't you? Look, I'm going ahead of you, slowly. It would be easy to reach out and—push. No? Ah well, there'll be another time, I daresay."

Levanah, reaching the lowest step, turned to smile up at her aunt and then walked through into the long drawing room. Leah, her face blank, followed, the skirt of her dress trailing limply over the stone.

The drawing room with its apricot hung French windows, its rugs of honey and cream, its gold and embossed sofas and wing chairs and its delicately molded ceiling was an elegant apartment. The round table was set for morning coffee and apple logs burned sweetly in the grate.

"Three cups?" Leah sat down in one of the chairs and looked an inquiry.

"I am expecting a visitor," her niece said. "You enjoy visitors, Aunt. I have often thought we ought to invite more people to Kingsmead."

"I dislike visitors," Leah said flatly.

"But this is a very special visitor, Aunt," Levanah smiled. "An old friend whom you haven't seen for years."

"Who?"

"Michael Shaw. You remember Michael Shaw, don't you? The gentleman to whom your sister rented her little cottage nearly thirty years ago? My father?"

"Michael Shaw here?" Leah's face had paled to a chalky white and her eyes were frightened.

"He sent a messenger over from the village a couple of hours ago," Levanah said. "Apparently he's been staying there for the past three days."

"But why has he come back?" Leah asked in agitation. "Why after all these years should he decide to come back?"

"A sentimental pilgrimage perhaps," Levanah said. "Or perhaps he's here to ask you a few questions, to talk over old times. He might wish to know why when he wrote to my mother to tell her that his wife was dead and he was free to marry her, you held back the letter and told my mother instead that Michael Shaw had died suddenly. And he might wish to know why after Beth killed herself, you wrote to him and told him she was dead but forgot to mention there had been a child."

"I told you," Leah said, licking her lips, "that I

was afraid he might claim you. He could never have
given you the advantages—"

"Of a Falcon upbringing? That's very true." Levanah laced her fingers together and smiled gently.
"And see how you have been rewarded for your
kindness! Mary has gone and Teddy is dead, and
here are you and I together at Kingsmead."

"I shall not remain to see him," Leah began, but
her niece's hand shot out and fastened upon her
wrist.

"It would be very rude not to see him after so
long a time," she said. "You are not afraid of him,
are you? Why, he must be in his seventies now. A
frail old gentleman visiting his widowed daughter.
He will be seeing his grandchildren too for the first
time if Johnny and Selena return before he leaves."

"I have a headache," Leah said.

"Then a cup of coffee may help to clear it," Levanah said calmly.

"I must tidy myself," Leah said, rising and wrench-
ing herself free.

"Yes, of course. Don't be too long, though, or I
may," said Levanah playfully, "come to fetch you."

She smiled again as her aunt hurried out. Then her
expression grew pensive. Perhaps it would be better
if she were to meet her father alone. It was nearly
ten years since she had gone to the studio in London
to inform him that his brief affair with Beth Falcon
had borne fruit. She had felt no particular emotion
upon meeting her father for the first time. He had
struck her as a lonely man, living on regrets for past
mistakes. But since receiving his note she had been
conscious of a faint warmth deep inside herself. It
might, after all, be pleasant to see him again. She had
read his name once or twice in the newspapers and

understood that he enjoyed some considerable reputation. Perhaps he felt the desire to be with someone who had loved the mother she had never known.

The doorbell pealed through the house and she jumped nervously, her fingers patting the hair smoothly over her ears. Mabel would answer it, and in a moment her father would come into the room. She could hear footsteps and the faint murmur of voices.

"Lady Falcon, Mrs. Falcon and Mr. Shaw to see you," Mabel said.

The welcoming smile died on her lips and her eyes were cold as she rose to greet them. Cousin Wenna had played no part in the imagined scene, but it was she who stepped forward now, saying, "Your father invited me to accompany him this morning. After such a long absence he thought the presence of a third party might ease the situation."

"You are very welcome at any time," Levanah said coolly, "but you don't often choose to visit Kingsmead, do you? Won't you both sit down?"

She nodded toward the sofa and sat down again herself, saying to Mabel, who hovered nearby, "We will need an extra cup, and you may bring in the coffee now and tell my aunt we are ready."

"My coming here must seem strange," Michael began.

"Not at all. One cannot expect such a busy man to have time to spare for rural folk," Levanah said.

She had grown from a hard young girl into a hard young woman, Michael thought. There was no warmth in the amber eyes and her long nails were curved like claws in the lap of her black dress. Against the deep rose of the high-backed chair her face had the pale purity of a cameo.

"I was very sorry to hear of your husband's death," he said.

"Yes. Poor Teddy." She spoke almost indifferently, her eyes still hard. "Wenna lost her husband on the same day, you know. We are a family without men now."

"But you have a son."

"And a daughter." Slight animation came into her face. "Johnny is very much like Teddy. Selena has red hair but a quieter temperament than one usually associates with that shade."

"I had hoped to meet them."

"Oh, you may do so as soon as they come in. You didn't walk from the village?"

"Wenna drove me over in the buggy," Michael said.

So it was Wenna! The yellow eyes flickered toward the older woman. Wenna had lost weight since her husband's death too, but her hips and bust were rounded as Levanah's had never been. Her hair was coiled round her ears and between the coils her face had the rosiness of an apple.

"It might be best if you were to be introduced to the children as an old friend of the family," Levanah said. "And I will call you Mr. Shaw."

He nodded, thinking wryly that two meetings in ten years hardly entitled him to be called "Father."

"Michael has been over in France," Wenna said.

"I didn't know civilians were permitted to travel."

"I was able to pull a few strings," he said. "I went over to see for myself what it was like, to try to record scenes that might reveal to those who had not seen them the realities of war."

"It's so deadly boring to even think of such

things," Levanah said. "The war has been a terrible inconvenience."

He remembered the long lines of refugees he had seen, the weary faces of the old peasant women, the bewilderment of the children, the ruined crops and shattered houses, the churning mud in which men and beasts struggled to move.

"It was certainly inconvenient for Teddy and Cal," Wenna said, with an edge to her voice.

"But it does no good to dwell on such unpleasant matters," Levanah said. "I do feel that it is our duty to be brave for the sake of our children. Ah! here is Mabel with the coffee. Thank you, Mabel. And Aunt Leah! Do you remember Aunt Leah?"

He had seen her once or twice during the summer he had stayed at the cottage, but he would not have recognized the slim, raven-haired young woman in this gray-haired black-clad figure. Bitterness was etched deeply into the white face and the dark eyes looked as if they had not closed in peaceful sleep for years.

"Mrs. Simmons." Bowing over her hand he reminded himself that this woman had separated him from Beth, had kept the knowledge of his daughter's existence from him. There had been moments when he had thought with burning hatred of this woman. Now the hatred had gone and he was conscious of nothing more than a faint disgust.

"It's been a very long time," Leah said.

"Almost thirty years," Levanah reminded them, pouring coffee. "Why, Uncle John was still alive when you were here. Teddy's father, you know. I was born the day after Uncle John died. And within the week my own mother had killed herself."

"It's an old tale," Wenna said. "Why bring it up now?"

"I wasn't seeking to embarrass anyone," Levanah said sweetly. "We all realize that Aunt Leah acted as she considered right. After all these years I'm sure that everything is forgiven and forgotten."

You, my daughter, are a bitch, Michael thought. *There is nothing in you of Beth, and I pray to God nothing of me.*

Aloud he said, "I came here to pay my respects to Beth's memory. I too had a share in the guilt of her death, so it's not for me to cast blame. She would not have wished it."

"You are very generous," Leah said, but she spoke sullenly as if she had nerved herself for an encounter and been cheated.

"Most generous!" Levanah echoed with a down-slanting smile.

"I have asked Michael if he will spend a few weeks at Whittle Farm with Giles and me," Wenna said into a little silence.

"Indeed?" Levanah's raised brows added the phrase, *So soon after your husband's death.*

"I have no ties to keep me in London," Michael said.

"But to stay here? Surely the memories are too painful," Levanah said.

"I was not planning to intrude upon you here," he said in rebuke.

"Oh, but you must visit us as often as you please!" Lavanah exclaimed. "Aunt Leah and I are very dull, buried in this big house."

"Here are the children," Leah said with something like relief in her voice.

The two who entered were slight and small, the

boy a more delicate version of Wenna's son, the girl
an elf with wistful gray eyes and a smooth cap of
shining red hair. They had been nicely brought up,
and shook hands politely, the girl bobbing a curtsy.

My grandchildren, Michael thought, watching
them as they accepted a biscuit each and went out
sedately as two elderly people. Their good behavior
lasted only as far as the hall, however. Michael was
amused to hear a scuffle, a slap and a childish voice
raised in temper.

"They're nice children," he said.

"Spoilt," said Leah. "I never allowed any of you
to squabble in such a fashion."

"Which may be why Mary left home as soon as
she possibly could," Levanah said.

Leah's face grew paler and she set down her cup
with a little clatter.

"I don't want to discuss Mary," she said shrilly.
"She made her own decision and she must live with
it."

"Did you know," Levanah addressed Michael,
"that my cousin Mary went off with a most peculiar
young woman? Charlotte Bishop, but she insisted on
being called Charlie."

"I said I didn't want to talk about her," Leah
said.

"Then we won't, Aunt dear. I was only trying to
bring our guest up to date on family affairs. There
really hasn't been much of anything new recently,
unless we count the recent sad events."

Her eyes mocked at Wenna for a moment.

"I loved Teddy very dearly," Leah said suddenly.
"I reared him after he was orphaned, reared him as
if he were my own, ran the estate on his behalf until

he came of age. I loved him very much. I mourn for him."

"We all mourn for him," Levanah said. "You seem to forget that I was his wife."

"We are none of us allowed to forget that," Leah said sullenly.

"My aunt," said Levanah, "always hoped that Teddy would marry Mary, but he fell in love with me instead."

She shaped a smile at the others and put down her own cup very gently.

"If you will excuse me, I'll go and see what the children are doing," Leah said. "It was—interesting to see you again, Mr. Shaw."

"My aunt," said Levanah, watching the black-garbed figure trail from the room, "is devoted to the twins. You are unfortunate in that respect, Cousin Wenna. Or perhaps I ought to say that Giles is unfortunate."

"In what way?" Wenna asked, drawing herself up slightly.

"I only meant that a widow is often apt to cling to an only son," Levanah said. "Of course you may be an exception."

"I hope so," Wenna said coldly. She glanced at Michael as she spoke and he rose, reaching for his hat and gloves, saying as cordially as he could, "We ought to be going. I had no intention of taking up the whole of your morning."

"And no doubt Cousin Wenna and you have plans of your own for the afternoon," said Levanah.

Her eyes were sly as the eyes of a fox. Michael disliked her eyes. If he stayed much longer he would dislike every part of his daughter intensely.

"You will give my love to Giles?" she was saying.

"He is such a shy, difficult boy. I try very earnestly to make friends whenever I see him, but he never has anything to say to me. You must think about sending him to school, Wenna. A little polish would make quite a gentleman of him."

"You're so good at giving advice, Levanah," Wenna said, smiling with a little snap in her voice.

They shook hands coldly and went out into the hall. Michael reflected that this was the first time he had ever been inside the great house, his summer of nearly thirty years before having been spent in the little cottage close to the river. In this house Beth had been born, had lived her nineteen years and had ended her life. He had always imagined that it would pain him to visit this place but there was nothing in him beyond a gentle regret for what might have been. Kingsmead was, he thought, too full of ghosts; strange, violent ghosts who jostled for his attention in every creaking panel, every rustling tapestry, every shadow that whispered in the corners. There was no room among them for the girl he had loved.

"Was it very painful for you to see Levanah again?" Wenna asked as they climbed up to the buggy.

She had given him the reins without asking him, as if it were natural for her to trust him. That pleased him.

"Levanah is—not a comfortable person," he said slowly.

"No. She is not—comfortable." Wenna hesitated, biting her lip. "She and Leah, living together in that house, hating each other. They do hate each other, you know."

"Leah reared her."

"Having driven her mother to suicide, and having kept her from her true father," Wenna said.

"She has no affection for me," Michael said dryly, "unless she hides it well."

"And you have none for her?"

He shook his head.

"It's too late. Two meetings in a whole lifetime—that isn't enough."

"And Leah? Do you hate Leah?"

He shook his head again.

"I am afraid of Levanah," Wenna said abruptly. "I don't know exactly why, but I am afraid of her. When she was a child there was a sweetness in her, and then she went away for a long time. And when she came back to marry Teddy, she was different. There was something at the back of her eyes—oh, I can't explain it! Teddy was in love with her. He used to stop by the farm and chat to Cal and me. It was always how wonderful Levanah was. He was so proud when she had Johnny and Selena."

"So?"

"I don't know," she said helplessly. "I can only tell you that ever since she came back I have felt a fear deep inside me. I used to see her sometimes walking in the village or standing on the bridge, staring down into the water. Just standing there. Smiling, you know. As if she were waiting. Odd, but I've not seen her do that since Cal and Teddy went."

"You read too much into things," he said uneasily.

"Perhaps. I only know that I keep Giles away from her and from the big house as much as I possibly can."

He gave her a sideways glance of concern. Her profile was downbent, the curve of her lips tremulous. The coils of hair about her ears irritated him. He had never liked to see a woman's hair pinned and plaited.

"You should wear your hair loose," he said abruptly.

"At my age?"

"At any age, if it suits you."

She began to pull the ivory-headed pins from her hair, to shake out the plaits. He slowed the horse to a walking pace and watched the slow, steady rhythm of her fingers. The hair, thick and brown, banded with silver, waved down her back. She thrust it aside and turned her face toward him. Her green eyes had a tranquil awareness.

"Do you want to take the reins?" he asked.

Wenna put out her hand, covering his own.

"We'll share them," she said, and her face glowed with a look that made September like the promise of April.

"Giles will be wanting his dinner," he said after a long moment. "And I still have his train to mend."

They both knew that more than a train had been mended.

Chapter 5

The peace had come and there had been flags and bunting and a party in the square with sticky buns and lemonade. Cat had been to the party but she had not enjoyed it very much. At eleven she was becoming more and more solitary in her habits. Her teachers complained that she spent too much time gazing out of the window, and at break, while the others played ball in the yard, she wandered about by herself, or sat on the low wall that divided yard from playing field, with her thin legs swinging and her eyes dreaming into space. There was no profit in scolding her, for the work she handed in was done well and neatly. And when her classmates urged her to join in their games she did so willingly enough, generally won and went off again with no sign of triumph or pleasure.

"Such an odd child! Not that one can blame her, living with that old woman! She needs young company around her."

"She's intelligent, mind. Very quick for her age, and speaks English as well as Welsh."

"Her mother was English, you know. A great-niece or something of old Mrs. Catrin's. She came here to have the child and then went away again. As to who the father was—I've no idea and I wouldn't care to inquire."

Cat had no interests in the remarks that other people made about her. She felt no particular yearnings for companionship or for a home such as other children had. She enjoyed being at Saron with her Aunt Catrin. It was hard work for a child for Aunt Catrin had grown old very rapidly in the past months and spent nearly all her time sleeping, so that Cat had to do a lot of cooking and cleaning. But she liked preparing meals and making the house tidy and she liked, most of all, the long evenings when the old woman sat in the rocking chair and rambled on in her cracked old voice, never expecting an answer, so that Cat was free to think her own thoughts.

She concentrated many of her thoughts on the mother she had never known. It seemed so odd for a mother to leave a pretty baby and go away and never come back. Cat thought too about her grandmother, the girl in the picture. She wondered if the girl, Beth, had loved her daughter, or if she had died before she had begun to feel any affection for the little thing. She thought too about the big house she had seen from time to time in the flames of the fire. She could describe the house in detail, from the walled courtyard with its arched entrance to the shallow steps that led up to the dark oak door with the diamond-paned windows set deep in their stone mullions. One day she would walk through that doorway and look up at the stone facade of the building! She knew that just as she knew that one day she would find the white cottage in the glade where the girl, Beth, had stood with bleeding wrists.

Meanwhile she went to school every day, riding on the docile pony that was the most reliable means of transport she had; and in the long evenings, when the work had been done and nobody bothered to tell her to go to bed, she slipped into her dreams. The conversations she had with the girl in the picture and the little carved figure were more interesting than anything her school friends had to say, and the things she saw in the crystal were far more real than the events that took place around her. In the apparent loneliness of the little farm she lived a secret life that was very far from lonely.

She had, during the summer months, formed a habit of taking a walk in the hours between tea and sunset. Aunt Catrin always fell asleep after tea, and rather than disturb her by the clattering of dishes, the child preferred to roam about in the fresh air until the deepening purple of the mountain warned her there was work waiting.

Sometimes she wandered to the edge of the farmland where meadow became marsh and the path twisted like a dark ribbon through the treacherous green. Sometimes she went farther afield, across the main road and up one of the side lanes between hedges thick with blackberries in early autumn, starred with meadowsweet in spring.

It was on one of these solitary rambles that she had pushed her way through a ring of tangled bushes into a circle of high grass in the midst of which was the broken rim of what had once been a well. The inside was almost silted up and over it drooped a tree with leaves such as she had never seen before. Each leaf was the color of rust, veined in purple, and when she crushed one a sweet, minty fragrance drifted to her nostrils. She thought of the tree as her magic tree and the well as her magic place, and shared it only with the occasional badger or rabbit. Once she had seen a fox near the well, its mask uplifted, its bushy tail feathering the long grass. It had stared at her for a moment out of yellow eyes in which there was a kind of recognition, and then slunk away. After that she often went to the well, sitting in the long grass, her own green eyes fixed on the shifting patterns of the leaves as the light wind tossed the branches of the tree.

The party over and the crowds dispersed, Cat had ridden home to tell Aunt Catrin about it. Not that the telling gave her much more satisfaction than the party had done, for the old woman became very confused as to which war had just ended, or even if there had been a war at all, and she had nodded to sleep even before Cat had begun to tell her about the silver sixpence each child had received. So Cat had put the sixpence into Aunt Catrin's lap and gone out into the warmth of the late afternoon.

The magic well beckoned her as if the branches of its attendant tree were threads drawing her into the circle of bushes. Halfway up the path she broke into a skipping run, her thick plaits bouncing at each side of her face, her legs thin and brown under the woolen skirt.

There was no sunlight in the green circle, but the rusty leaves were tipped with gold. Cat sank down into the grass, which was cool and damp even on the hottest day, and laced her fingers together. Closing her eyes she lifted her head to the rustling of the leaves and let peace wash over her.

When she opened her eyes again a lady was standing before her. The woman must have approached through the bushes on the other side of the well, but she had made no sound. Cat stared up at her, feeling nothing but a vague surprise, and the woman stared back gravely.

She was not a tall woman, but her statuesque figure and the long, smock dress she wore gave the impression that she was above average height. Her blue eyes and the heavy blond hair coiled at the back of her head were youthful, but her voice was tired and husky as if she had lived too long and seen too much.

"Good day. Do you speak English?"

"Yes. I speak it well. Most folk hereabouts do."

The woman sat down on the rim of the well and went on looking at her. The dress she wore had a pattern of green and brown leaves blurred thickly over a creamy background. She blended into her surroundings and there was a quietness about her that soothed the child.

"Do you have a name?"

"Catrin Falcon. I'm known as Cat because my aunt is Catrin too."

"Do you live with this aunt?"

Cat nodded, volunteering, "She is a great-great something aunt, past ninety."

"Have you no parents?"

Cat shook her head, pulling a long stalk of grass and nibbling its sap-sweet end.

"My name is Leone," the woman said. "Leone Starbeck, but you may call me Leone. Can you guess why I was called that?"

"No. I never heard the name before."

"I was born in August, under the sign of Leo. My

parents studied such things. That is why they called me Leone. When is your birthday?"

"Early in March."

"Pisces, the sign of the fishes," the woman nodded. "And have you no brothers or sisters?"

"Just Aunt Catrin."

The woman nodded again and a little silence fell between them, a space in which each took the other's measure.

"And you come here to play?" Leone said at last.

"I come here to think."

"Of what were you thinking when I came?"

"Of the war," Cat said slowly. "We had a party, you know, because the Germans have signed a treaty, in France somewhere."

"At Versailles."

"Yes, somewhere like that. There was a party with jellies and flags and a band and yet all the people in the war are still dead." Cat's green eyes were puzzled. "All those men killed and now the people laughing. It made no sense to me."

"You think they should weep forever?" Leone looked at her wryly. "I thought that too, for a little while. Both my sons were killed in Flanders a few months after my husband died. I believed then that I would weep forever. But one doesn't, you know. One goes on."

"Are you a visitor then?" Cat asked.

"I have sufficient money to travel a little. I indulge myself."

"Are you staying here? I thought people generally stayed in Caernarvon."

"I stopped off in Bangor to look at the cathedral. I've walked from there. I like walking."

Her feet were encased in sensible shoes and her

dress was of a warm, serviceable stuff. About her eyes and mouth were lines of humor and endurance. There was a stability about her that struck some chord of need in the child's own nature.

"And you found my private place," she said.

'I hope you don't mind my trespassing, but the world is so tame these days, so coffined in hedges that I like to explore the wilder parts."

"It's not very wild," Cat said doubtfully. "The Evans' farm is over the rise, and my school is only three miles down the main road. I won the scholarship, you know, a whole year before anyone is supposed to win it. And this is just an old well."

"A very ancient one." Leone bent and scraped at the moss. "There are runes here, cut deeply into the stone. This is a pre-Christian well. A sacrificial one probably. Can you not imagine how it once was?"

"I can see it behind my eyes," Cat said frowning. "Women with a strange mark on their foreheads, hair bound with colored ribbons, holding sticks in their hands. Chanting, chanting."

"Derfel women of the old fertility cult," Leone said nodding. "Did you read about them in school?"

"They don't teach us interesting things like that in school," Cat said regretfully. "I see them, like when I look in the crystal."

"Crystal?" Leone's blue eyes were intent.

"My mother left it for me when she went away," Cat said.

"She's not dead then?"

"She came from England and had me here," the little girl confided. "After I was born she went away again and left me with Aunt Catrin. But she left me the crystal, and when I look into it I can see things."

"Only when you look into it?"

"I see things at other times too," Cat said. "And then at school they shout 'Cat Falcon! What is so interesting outside the window?' It's not what's outside the window that I see, but what's there behind my eyes when the air gives a little shiver."

Leone was still studying her intently. Her hand, resting on the mossy stone, was very tense. A ring glowed purple on the forefinger and sent back gleams of light.

"Does your aunt have the 'seeing'?" she asked.

"She said there were other women in the family who could do it. Witch women."

"You don't remember your parents then?"

Cat shook her black head. "I am," she said sorrowfully, "an abandoned child."

"With an aunt to take care of you, and a place in school, and a crystal ball? Fiddlesticks!"

"I have a ring too," Cat said proudly. "A moonstone ring. It belonged to my grandmother. She had her picture painted with it on."

"Do you like my ring?" Leone held out her hand toward the child.

Cat put out her finger and touched the gleaming stone. Under her skin the jewel throbbed and burned like a living thing.

"It is like the well," she said at last. "Old, very old, but still young."

"It goes on from age to age," Leone said, "but the power is not in the ring. It is in the person. And much depends on how we use that power."

Cat had only the vaguest notion of what she was talking about, but the words reached some part of herself beyond reason or conscious thought. She wanted Leone to go on talking, for the sound wove a tapestry about her and in the tapestry were threads of singing color.

The woman had stopped however and had risen. From where she still sat in the long grass Cat said, "Won't you come back and have a bite of supper with Aunt Catrin and me? It's not far and we've plenty to spare."

"I was hoping you'd ask me," Leone said.

Cat was suddenly happy, so happy that tears pricked her eyelids. Her moods often went by contraries, her disappointment bubbling into laughter, her joy dissolving into tears. At this moment she was in love with the whole world, and because she was too small to encompass the world she felt tears of bitter frustration.

"Lead the way then," her new friend invited, and she sprang up, quivering, and darted through the bushes into the lane.

Saron Farm drowsed in the sunset. From a distance it looked like an illustration from a calendar of country scenes. As one drew closer it became apparent that the property was badly neglected. The house needed several coats of whitewash, there were cracked panes in two of the windows and many slates were missing from the roof.

"We have a boy who comes every day to work the land," Cat said, opening the gate. "He goes home after the cow is milked. I generally wash the tea things and make a bit of supper for when Aunt Catrin wakes up. She's asleep much of the time, you know, and when she's awake she doesn't always make much sense."

The room into which Cat led the woman was commendably neat and tidy, the dishes stacked up in the stone sink, the fire glowing low. The woman who sat in the rocking chair was very old, her back bent, a shawl covering her thin white hair, spectacles perched on the end of her nose. She had evidently just woken up, for her voice was slurred with the remnants of a dream.

"Levanah mustn't be told. That's important. She would be angry if she knew I had kept the child."

"Aunt Catrin, I've brought a lady home," Cat said loudly.

"Mrs. Catrin? My name is Leone Starbeck." She too raised her voice slightly as she bent to grasp the thin hand.

"From England? You've not come to take Cat away, have you?"

"She's come to tea," Cat said.

"They all go into England and get married," Aunt Catrin said testily. "They marry their Falcon cousins, you know, and never come back. My own girl, Wenna, went into England and married a Falcon cousin."

"He was killed in the war, Aunt," Cat reminded her. "She's married to someone else now. Don't you remember you had a letter from her at Christmas?"

"She sends money to me," the old woman said proudly, "and a letter every few months. To me, of course, for nobody knows about Cat."

"I've always been a secret," Cat said, busying herself at the sink. "My mother told Aunt Catrin to put me in the orphanage. None of the others know about me."

"The others?" Tactfully refraining from offering help to the child, Leone sat down on a chair next to the old woman.

"The Falcons," Aunt Catrin said. "My niece, Margred, went into England and wed a Falcon, and my own girl wed a Falcon, and Margred's granddaughter wed a Falcon, and now they will take my Cat away. You must promise not to tell."

"I'll not tell," said Leone.

"They've left me alone," said Aunt Catrin, with a snort of satisfaction. "They don't come here. They send money to salve their consciences and I put it aside to keep for her. That'll fox them!"

She clasped her hands tightly together, winked in an unexpectedly roguish manner and said, as if Leone too were deaf, "I want my supper, Cat! Lots of bara-brith and a bit of ham. Do you like ham?"

"Very much," Leone assured her.

"Jews don't," said Aunt Catrin. "They don't like ham, I'm told. I brought Cat up to have more sense."

"You brought her up very well," Leone said. "She must be a very great help to you now."

"But it's not right," said Aunt Catrin, her old face crumpling into a bewildered grief. "It's not right that the old should suck the young dry. It bothers me, for what will happen to her when I'm gone? The Falcons will come and take her and she'll never come back."

"Now don't go upsetting yourself," Cat warned. To Leone she said, "She worries, you know. She worries about what will happen to me when she's gone."

"It's natural." Leone watched the child set out plates and mugs on the table, moving briskly and gracefully, her hands and face intent on her task.

"I shall go into England one day," Cat said in a low voice not designed to reach the old woman, "and find my mother. I'd not be a trouble to her, but I'd like to know why she went away and told Aunt Catrin to put me in an orphanage. Do you think a traveling man stopped by?"

"A traveling man?"

"Aunt Catrin's sister had a baby after a traveling man stopped by," Cat said. "The baby grew up to be my great-grandmother."

"My mother was a Falcon," said Aunt Catrin, so suddenly that the other two jumped, afraid she had overheard. "And *her* mother was a Falcon too. Apple Falcon. She's buried on this land next to her husband. And my mother lies with them. Died up at the old well she did, when Saran and I were girls."

"The old well?" Cat brought a mug of tea over to the old woman. "You mean the old well here?"

"No, no. Up the road a way. She used to go there, walking alone, but her breathing was bad. They found her there one morning crouched over. Funny, but the night before, Saran saw the death candle out on the marsh. It was all marshy then, and the road was narrower. Now it's all houses and smelly motor cars, and they say men will be flying in the air soon. I don't believe it myself, but then people will say anything to create a sensation."

"Drink your tea," Cat said. She had beckoned Leone to the table and now began to ladle honey into an earthenware pot. "She rambles on, you know," she said, lowering her voice again. "But I didn't hear about her mother being found dead at the well before. I wonder if that's why I like the place. The dead don't frighten me, you know."

"No reason why they should." Leone sank her teeth into the crusty bread. "And your aunt doesn't ramble. She is coming round full circle back to her childhood again, that's all. I take it that her sister died and she reared the child?"

"Until Margred went into England to marry her cousin," Cat nodded. "Aunt Catrin was married herself once too, you know, and she had a daughter, Wenna."

"The one who sends the money?"

Cat nodded as Aunt Catrin demanded, from her seat by the fire, "What are you muttering about?"

"I was telling Leone about your Wenna," Cat said loudly.

"Married young did Wenna," said Aunt Catrin. "He was killed in the quarry before the year was out. She'd not the heart to stay here then, so she went off into England and, years later, she married one of the Falcons. Years older than him she was, but she wrote and told me they were happy."

"He was killed," Cat reminded her.

"That's right. Killed in a war or some such thing," Aunt Catrin agreed. "One war after another. But Wenna caught herself another husband. She wrote and told me about it. She sends money for me, and I keep it for Cat. This farm will be Wenna's when I go, but my savings are for Cat."

"You're dripping your tea," Cat said, hurrying to her aunt's side.

"I'm sleepy," the old woman said abruptly. "I'll have a nap before I go to bed."

She suited action to words, dropping her chin on her chest, her glasses slipping farther down her nose.

"She never had her ham," Cat said regretfully. "She does enjoy a bit of ham since she had her new teeth put in. Will you have another cup?"

"No thank you." Leone pushed back her chair. "I ought to be on my way. It's getting later than I thought, and I imagine it's a good step down to Caernarvon. I left my cases in Bangor at the station, but I suppose a hotel will let me register without luggage. Shall I help you with the old lady?"

"She'll be awake again as soon as I start clearing the dishes," Cat said. "After that she may stay awake till near midnight. I go to bed after I've settled her."

It was, thought the older woman with a pang of pity, no life for a child.

"If there was a spare room," she said impulsively, "I'd beg a bed for the night."

"There are two bedrooms," Cat said, "but you can share mine if you like. I can use the little truckle bed. We keep it for visitors, but we've never had any up to now."

"I can take the spare bed, if it's no trouble," Leone said.

"I'd be glad of the company," Cat said, unconscious pathos in her eager face. "You could stay longer if you'd a mind—or do you have to go home soon?"

A vision of her house with its mute reminders of husband and sons rose up in Leone Starbeck's mind.

"If your aunt doesn't object—", she began.

"Aunt Catrin likes what I like," said the girl. "Come and see the room!"

She lifted one of the oil lamps from the dresser and opened one of the two doors on the left.

The bedroom was neat, clean and indefinably shabby. Leone's eyes were drawn to the flat-topped tallboy on which the crystal, the little carved figure and the portrait were ranged. In the soft light the objects glowed as if they waited to illumine some dark corner of the mind. For an instant Leone shivered as if a cold finger had touched her spine.

"Do you like the room?" Cat was asking. "The

girl in the picture is my grandmother, Beth, and the ring on her hand is the one my mother left for me."

Leone's blue eyes regarded the painted eyes. The amethyst on her forefinger flashed as she briefly raised her hand. All she said was, "I'll help you with the dishes."

Chapter 6

"I think," said Charlie Bishop, "that it all looks madly gay!"

"Madly gay" was her latest expression, to be used indiscriminately on every occasion. The apartment with its black walls, white furniture and vivid cushions did, however, merit the term. A gold and silver mobile danced endlessly above the cocktail bar and an arrowed sign pointed coyly to the bathroom. It was smart and modern and wildly expensive, but Charlie's latest book had made her a great deal of money.

She had begun writing while they were living in Switzerland during the war and it was hard to make ends meet with pupils growing fewer. Her essays on life in a neutral country had been gay and satirical, with just the right amount of homesick fervor to appeal to expatriate Britons. On their return to London Charlie had settled down in earnest to earn both their livings by the brightly malicious use of her pen. A collected volume of her wartime pieces, a playscript, two syndicated columns in a couple of the more popular newspapers and a faintly risqué novel had brought comparative affluence in a very short space of time.

Charlie herself now dressed the part of a successful author—red velvet trousers and smock vying with her scarlet-tinted hair. Horn-rimmed spectacles, an ivory holder through which she puffed incessantly at black Russian cigarettes and a long rope of cheerfully artificial pearls completed the picture.

She cast a satisfied look at herself in the gilt-framed pier glass as she went past it. The party was due to begin within the hour and twenty people had accepted, which meant that at least twice that number would expect drinks and snacks.

"Ladislas, that lovely boy from the new comedy, has promised to bring some Polish friends with him," she said. "I wonder if they will all be moody and Slavonic."

"Probably."

"As long as they don't cramp everyone else's style. Do you remember that perfectly dreadful young man who sat on the floor and positively bawled over the wrongs done to his country? And we never did find out exactly where he came from!"

"Yes."

"You might show a little more interest in what I'm saying," Charlie complained. "Honestly, darling, I've been working my fingers to the bone, and all you can do is to sit there with a dazed expression on your face!"

"I'm sorry," Mary said. "It all looks very—madly gay, Charlie."

"I must run down to Francini's," Charlie said, "and see if they've kept the champagne on ice. You will amuse yourself while I'm gone, won't you? You won't sink into one of your depressions, will you?"

"No, no, I won't," Mary said vaguely. Charlie gave her an exasperated look, shrugged on a loose cloak and went out.

Mary rose from the low couch where she had been sitting and, wandering over to the pier glass, gazed at her reflection thoughtfully. Like Charlie she had cut her hair and it curled darkly over her small head, the side bangs held in place by a diamanté ribbon. Her chiffon dress, with its low waistline, was the latest style from Paris. It scarcely covered the knees in front but drooped behind into an ankle-length train looped with diamanté ribbon. Her shoes were buckled and long strands of coral hung about her neck. She looked, she decided, sweetly feminine. Franz had told her that she was the prettiest thing he had ever seen. He had held her closely, kissing her eyelids, her mouth, her ears, telling her he would never rest until she agreed to marry him. The feel of his lips against her own flesh had roused her to trembling excitement, but she had evaded his plea, had forced herself to move away, to speak lightly, mockingly.

"I'm past thirty, Franz. A confirmed spinster."

"You are the woman who will bear my children," he had answered.

"I have to think, Franz. I have to consider so many things."

"Is it that my father was German? He was not in the Army, and I also was not there. For him was a reserved occupation and for me one leg shorter than the other." He glanced ruefully at his thick-soled boot. "Is it that you dislike?"

"No, oh no! I would marry you gladly, Franz, but it's—"

"It's Charlie, isn't it?" His hands dropped to his sides and he spoke bitterly. "You don't want to leave her. You'll spend the rest of your life with that—woman, and turn your back on all that is true and good and normal!"

"Charlie is devoted to me," Mary said. "You don't know how much I owe to her! I was wretched at home with no life at all of my own beyond what my mother allowed me, and then Charlie asked me to go and live with her. She set me free."

"She invited you to step into another prison," he said.

"That's not fair! We've traveled all over the Continent together, and this apartment—she's worked so hard for it."

"I too can work hard. I intend to get a post as schoolteacher, and I'm already applying for naturalization papers. My mother was English, so it will not be difficult for me. I think I will take the 'von' out of my name, and be plain 'Braun.'"

"It's not that—you don't understand these things!"

"I understand it is not good for a woman to be without the man she loves," he said. "I understand that it is not good for a woman to be without the children Nature intended her to bear."

"If Charlie could live with us?" she suggested.

"If we marry it will be you and me," he interrupted-ed. "Charlie must make her own life."

"We ought to wait a little, to be quite sure of our feelings," she pleaded.

"I am quite certain of my feelings," he said, "and you cannot expect me to wait for the rest of my life.

I am thirty-five years old and I want a wife, a home, children. It is cruel of you not to answer me."

"Give me a little time, a few days."

"A few only," he said, "and then I will come for you and tell Charlie myself."

Tonight she was expecting him to come. Tonight she would have to tell Charlie that the quiet gentleman with the slight limp and the faint accent, whom she had met at the library, was far more than a friend. Charlie would be terribly angry. At the thought of Charlie's anger Mary began to shake a little.

She sat down again and reached out for the newspaper on the coffee table. Charlie's column was on the third page, but she had already read and praised it. She turned the pages idly, her eyes skimming the words in an effort to stop her tormented thoughts.

An item leapt out, claiming her attention.

Lord John Falcon, ten-year-old son of the late Lord Edward Falcon, yesterday unveiled a memorial to the memory of those who lost their lives in the recent hostilities. Seventeen men from the village of Marie Regina were among those who died in the service of their country. The memorial, a bronze pillar surmounted by a crown, was contributed to by subscription. Among those witnessing the ceremony were Lady Levanah Falcon, widow of Lord Edward, and Miss Selena Falcon, Lord John's twin sister. Also present were Mrs. Leah Simmons, Mrs. Michael Shaw, the former Wenna Falcon, and her son, Master Giles Falcon. Mrs. Shaw's late husband, Mr. Caleb Falcon, also lost his life in the war.

There was more of it, but the print had blurred and the newspaper slipped down to her lap. Names she had not seen or heard for years buzzed in her brain, and faces floated up to match the names.

Cal Falcon she had almost loved, but her mother had wanted her to marry Teddy. And in the end Cal had married Cousin Wenna and Teddy had married Levanah. She had remembered Levanah's red hair and narrow yellow eyes, and the soft chanting of her voice as she had raised a candle up to the tiny, carved figure.

"His name is Lob and he is the guardian of Witch's Dower," Levanah had said, and Cal and Mary had stood close in the candlelight, half-believing. But they had been discovered and Levanah sent away to London, and life at Kingsmead had become so unbearable that Mary had turned more and more to Charlie for affection, until, in the end, she had run away with her.

She picked up the paper and read the news item again. All these years of traveling and trying not to think of Kingsmead, and suddenly the years were swept away. Teddy had married Levanah and she had borne twins, and Cousin Wenna had married Cal and had a son called Giles.

She looked round the vivid room, and it was garish and tasteless with nothing in it to rest the eye or soothe the heart. The great hall at Kingsmead was the grayness of faded tapestries, the sheen of silver against dark oak, the warmth of sunlight striking through the mullioned windows.

If she looked out of the window of the apartment she could see the roofs of other buildings, with the smoke of the city hanging like a menace over slate and brick. From the windows of Kingsmead she had looked out across the meadows tall with corn and hops to woods where foxes and the occasional deer still roamed, and the river ran like a ribbon between banks heavy with irises and reeds. There had been much unhappiness for her at Kingsmead, but there had been sunlit days too when she had been the pretty girl from the big house, growing up with her cousins, Teddy and Levanah. She had thought to escape her mother's domination, but the place of her birth dominated her more subtly, and the urge to return grew in her like hunger.

The party, like most of Charlie's parties, was noisy and gay. The beautiful Ladislas brought the promised Poles; there were several White Russians, an actress who had recently been involved in a divorce case and a sprinkling of people on the fringes of the literary world. Everybody called everybody else "darling," ostrich feather fans were much in evidence and the hooting of taxicabs in the street below mingled with the laughter and chatter to produce a cacophony of gay discords.

"You look tired." Franz, leaning against the kitchen door, made the remark gently.

"I'm bored," Mary said. Her own words startled her a little and she considered them, the cloth with which she was wiping dishes hanging idle between her fingers. "It's true," she said, after a moment's reflection. "I am most horribly bored."

"So you will consider marrying me as an antidote to boredom?"

"Would you take me on those terms?"

"I think so," he said slowly. "Love would come later perhaps."

"I love you now," she said quickly. "But to marry

me— Franz, I come from a very strange family, you know."

"How can I know since you never speak of them?"

"My mother was Leah Falcon," she said. "The Falcons are an old Kentish family. The eldest son was granted a hereditary peerage by Charles the Second, and we've always owned land and a big house. My mother was widowed before I was born, and at about the same time her brother, Lord John, died, so his boy Teddy was brought up with me."

"What is so strange about that?"

"I had two other cousins," she said. "My mother had two younger sisters and they both had children out of wedlock. Aunt Edith had a boy named Cal and they lived at Whittle Farm on the other side of the river. We were not supposed to play with Cal. Aunt Beth had a little girl and died, so Levanah was brought up with Teddy and me."

"I still see nothing strange," he remarked.

"Levanah owned a little cottage down by the river," Mary said, and unconsciously she shivered. "Witch's Dower it's always been called. There's a story that a Falcon once married a woman out of Wales, a strange girl with yellow eyes and the mark of a crescent moon on her thigh. From time to time there have been women with Welsh blood in our family."

"So?"

"Levanah had yellow eyes and the mark of a crescent moon on her thigh," Mary whispered. "She was little and red-haired and I was always fond of her, but I feared her too. She was so little and quiet, but I always did what she wanted me to do. She took me down to the little cottage and we had—she called them rituals."

"What kind of rituals?"

"I don't know. She had a little wooden figure that Cal made for her, and a crystal ball, and the picture of a girl. She lit candles before them and chanted. She could make the flames of the candles go up and down just by looking at them, and she could make the wind blow."

"Nonsense!"

"It is not nonsense," she insisted. "I don't know how she did it, but she could do it. It was frightening, but I didn't want to leave. Can you understand that?"

He nodded, his eyes on her slender fingers as they pleated the edges of the drying-up cloth.

"We were found out," Mary said. "My mother found out and there was the most terrible row. She called us heathens and pagans. I was forbidden to see Cal again and Levanah was sent away. I haven't seen her since. I spent all my time with Charlie. She taught at the village school with Wenna. I went everywhere with Charlie after Levanah was sent away. My mother didn't like that either. She tried to put a stop to it. In the end Charlie and I left."

"Why are you telling me this now?" Franz asked.

"I'm not certain. Yes, I am! I saw an item in the newspaper today. All the names I've not spoken, the faces I've tried to forget—Franz, Cal and Teddy were killed in the war. They were both killed and I never even knew. They both died."

"That must have been a shock," he said carefully.

"But the newspaper said that they'd both been married. Cal had married Cousin Wenna—she was years older than he was, but she had a son, it seems. A boy called Giles. And Teddy married Levanah and she had twins, a boy and a girl. Isn't that odd? Both of them married, and fathers, and dead, and I never knew. Life going on without me, Kingsmead and the village still there. When I read it I felt—I felt as if I were the one who had died."

She had begun to shake uncontrollably and tears beaded her lashes.

Franz limped over and put his arms about her. Against his shoulder she spoke jerkily.

"I was so pretty and I liked babies. My mother tried to push me off on Teddy, but he never wanted me, and I never thought of him as anything more than a cousin. And in the end, after I left, everything went on without me. Levanah and Wenna were the ones who married and had babies."

"You will bear my children," said Franz. "You will marry me and bear my children, and I will take you back to your house, to Kingsmead, if you wish."

"So that's the way of it."

Charlie, mouth smiling, eyes angry, stood in the doorway. Mary sprang away and began to dry glasses again, her cheeks scarlet.

Charlie closed the door and leaned against it, her eyes moving from one to the other.

"You seem to have been very busy," she said. "How clever of you to keep it from me for so long!"

"I mean to marry her," Franz said, "I mean to give her children, to take care of her."

"So you have it written out in your mind and signed, have you? A lame schoolteacher with a German name and large ideas!"

"You may insult if you choose," he said, "but you cannot prevent it."

"My dear man!" Charlie blew a smoke ring and

watched it. "Mary is a grown woman, free to do as she chooses. You don't see any bolts on the door, do you?"

"There are other bolts," he said.

"If you mean ties of affection," Charlie said, "those too can be severed. I have no wish to hold Mary against her will. I never have tried to hold her against her will."

"I never meant to hurt you," Mary sobbed. "I'll never forget what I owe to you, but Franz is—"

"I can give her children," Franz said, brutally gentle.

There was a long pause. Only the music and laughter came faintly through the door. Charlie blew another smoke ring, watched it blur into nothingness, and then nodded several times.

"I'm sorry," Mary said helplessly. "Oh, Charlie, I'm so sorry!"

"More than ten years," Charlie said, and her face twisted with bitter pain. "It's as long as a marriage."

She gave Franz a long look and abruptly flung open the door. Her voice shrilled across the room.

"Quiet, people! Everybody quiet! Darlings, I have the most marvelous news for you all! Mary and Franz are going to be married. There now! Isn't it all madly gay?"

They surged into the kitchen, flinging out congratulations and exclamations of surprise. Someone was opening a bottle of champagne. Charlie's voice went on and on.

"By special license at the end of the week. Yes, we have kept it a tremendous secret, but Mary and Franz didn't want a lot of fuss. Me? I'm delighted about it. I couldn't be more pleased if I were marrying him myself."

More laughter, more toasts. Franz and Charlie both kissing her and then kissing each other. The room was full of smoke and her head ached. The colors of the room hurt her eyes and the mobile chattered at her from above the cocktail bar. Nothing was quite real, and she surrendered to the fantasy, sipping champagne, accepting kisses, laughing, with Franz's arm about her and Charlie blowing endless smoke rings into the air.

A week later, wearing a cream dress that Charlie had picked out for her, with a lace veil under a close-fitting cap of orange blossoms, Mary was wed to Franz von Braun. It didn't seem like a real wedding at all, for there was no music or flowers. A single orchid pinned to the low waistband of her gown was smarter, Charlie had said, than a bouquet.

Charlie had arranged everything from the single-tier cake with the silver bells on top of it to the luncheon at the apartment.

"Nothing formal, darling, just a cold buffet for people to pick at! I'm rushing off to Paris next week so this all fits in perfectly with my plans! And only a few guests, darling. A couple of intimate friends, with the teeniest discreet announcement in my column."

"Nothing about the Falcons or Kingsmead," Mary had begged.

"Not one word. Your mother's husband was a Simmons, wasn't he?"

Mary Simmons, spinster, to Franz von Braun, bachelor.

She had plucked up the courage to say, at the last moment when Charlie was fixing the short lace veil into place, "I'm sorry. Truly I'm sorry."

And Charlie had said, "Sorry to be getting married? What a foolish thing to say, darling! Now do you honestly think I don't look *too* silly in a skirt? One gets so used to trousers."

It was over, and she had a thin gold band on her finger next to the half-hoop of diamonds that Franz had given her. They were going to Edinburgh for a week, and then Franz would go back to his teaching, and she would live with him in the cramped lodgings where the rooms always smelled of cabbage water.

"You're welcome to live here," Charlie had said gaily. "Lots of room, and I'm away half the time!"

"We intend to begin by ourselves," Franz had said.

"But of course you'll be welcome to come at any time to see us," Mary had said placatingly.

Now the guests were crowding about her, laughing, talking, sipping champagne. It was, Mary thought, as if the party of the previous week had simply continued, with the actual wedding ceremony constituting only a brief interruption.

"Quiet everybody! Quiet, please!" somebody was declaiming. "Charlie wants to make a speech!"

There was an outburst of clapping in the midst of which Ladislas was heard to mutter audibly, "But, sweetie, isn't it the *husband* who generally does the talking!"

Mary fixed her eyes on Charlie. Her friend looked handsome in lilac coat and skirt with a cloche hat pulled down over her short hair.

"Ladies and gentlemen, there isn't much left for me to say on this occasion except to wish bride and groom a long and happy life together," Charlie said clearly. "Mary and I have been together for a long time, and we have been contented and comfortable."

She   paused, her eyes seeking Mary, a mocking little smile on her lips.

"I was surprised," she said lightly, "that after all our years together Mary chose to get married, but she had every right, and true friendship doesn't seek to possess, only to give. Which reminds me that I haven't yet given Franz and Mary a wedding present."

"Oh, but we didn't expect anything," Mary protested.

"Nonsense, darling!" Everybody expects something," Charlie said gaily. "And I have the perfect going-away gift for you both."

"It's very kind of you," Franz said, frowning a little. The others had fallen silent and were staring at Charlie. Ice tinkled in a glass.

"Freedom," said Charlie, and her mouth was a clown's mouth. "I give you complete and absolute freedom, darlings. No ties!"

In the puzzled and uneasy silence she blew a kiss, turned to the wide-open window and jumped over the low sill. From the street below there came a muffled thud, and then somebody screamed on a high, piercing note.

People were crowding to the window and leaning out. Someone else had flung open the door and was clattering down the stairs. A police whistle sounded.

Mary, shaking within the circle of her bridegroom's arm, said loudly and childishly, "I want to go home! Oh, I want to go home!"

"We will go at once to my rooms," Franz comforted.

But she shook her head over and over and said, "I want to go home to Marie Regina! I want to go home to Kingsmead!"

Chapter 7

They had arrived the previous day and taken a taxi-cab to the Manor School. In the train Mary had told Franz something of the history of it.

"Years and years ago there was a manor house on the site. It became part of the Falcon estate through marriage, but it was burned down sometime last century. My mother used her own money to build a school for the village children where the house had stood. She called it the Lady Margred School after my grandmother, but nobody bothered to use the name. It's always been the Manor School."

It had been too dark to see the countryside and a cold wind had rattled the windows of the cab. Little Sigrid, wrapped in shawls, had whimpered as if something disturbed her dream.

"Kingsmead is on the left," Mary said, as they drove down the main road. "You can't see the house from here. The village is over on the right in the hollow between the graveyard and the hill. Can you see the outlines of the old monastery? This is the bridge. The entrance to the Manor School is just at the other side."

She was craning to see, a curious mixture of dread and anticipation on her face. Franz wondered yet again if he had done the right thing in applying for the vacant post of schoolmaster in this place where Mary had spent her childhood and from which she had fled. But the advertisement had come almost like a sign, when the birth of their child had meant they would soon have to seek new accommodations, and Mary's nightmares had become so frequent that the doctor advised country air.

"I can't forget Charlie," she said now, as the cab turned in through open gates. "I can't forget that awful thud. How could she do such a thing?"

"Because she had lost her love," he said somberly, "but it was her choice, *Liebchen*. You cannot blame yourself."

"I suppose not." She shivered and then said brightly, "This is the school. It was built before I was born."

It was difficult to see much but a white bulk of stone set in a green lawn with bushes and flower beds dotted about.

"The letter informed me the door would be unlatched," Franz said when they had emerged from the cab and he had paid the fare.

"The classroom is on the left and the cloakroom is on the right," said Mary. "There's always an oil lamp on the table just inside."

"Oil lamps in 1921!" Franz exclaimed.

"My mother never liked things to change," Mary said. "I believe she was getting up the courage to have gas installed at Kingsmead, but I left before she did anything about it. The flat is up the stairs ahead of you."

He held the lamp high to light her way as she went up with Sigrid in her arms. The cases, he decided, could be brought up later.

Upstairs the rooms were neat and clean, with no traces of the former occupants, two maiden ladies, according to the letter Franz had received, who had retired to Maidstone. The letter had been written by Lady Levanah Falcon in a curious, back-slanting script, the signature an ornate flourish. The letter had smelled of musk.

"A big living room, kitchen with food in the cupboard, two bedrooms, a bathroom." He checked with Germanic thoroughness.

Mary, standing in the middle of the living room, said, her voice trembling, "I used to come here to see Cousin Wenna and Charlie. Sometimes I used to help with the children. Charlie was a good teacher. She and Cousin Wenna weren't a bit alike but they worked well together."

"I'll bring up the cases," he said briskly, "and get the fire started. There's fresh milk in the kitchen, so you can warm some for the babe."

He had been relieved to see the color come back into her face, and the dangerous moment had passed. That night she had slept peacefully without twitching or moaning.

They had eaten breakfast and Mary was washing dishes in the tiny kitchen when hoofbeats sounded on the drive below. Franz, glancing through the window, had a brief flash of a black-clad figure alighting from the saddle. Then the front door opened and footsteps ran lightly up the stairs.

It was, he guessed, Levanah Falcon. Mary had

described her well. The light red hair curved toward
the narrow face at the level of the pointed jaw; the
yellow eyes slanted under the thick fringe. Her black
riding habit was softened by a jabot of white lace.
On the forefinger of her left hand a black pearl set in
gold gleamed. A diamond solitaire overshadowed the
wedding ring on her third finger and matched the
earrings dangling from her lobes.

What Mary had not described was the scent of
musk that rose from her, the thick yellow lashes that
cast faint shadows on her high cheekbones, the voice
that suggested more than it said as she glided forward.

"Mr. von Braun, I am Lady Falcon. I trust that
you and your wife found everything to your liking.
As school does not reopen after the half-term holiday
until Monday, that gives us a chance to become better acquainted."

"Lady Falcon." He bowed, aware of amusement in
the yellow eyes. Amusement, and something else that
eluded him.

Mary came out of the kitchen and the yellow eyes
widened for an instant. The voice lost its intimate
note and became light and hard.

"Mary? Cousin Mary! Don't tell me you have the
honor to be *Mrs.* von Braun—or should I say 'Frau'?"

"I am, as I told you in my letter of application,
of an English mother," Franz said. "I wish to apply
for naturalization."

"But you didn't tell me you were married to my
cousin Mary," said the light, amused voice. "You
look very well, Mary. Very well indeed."

"You haven't changed," Mary said.

"My dear, I am thirty-two years old," Levanah
said. "Positively an old hag! And you're married!

The last I heard of you you'd eloped with Charlotte Bishop. What happened to her? I thought you two were set for life."

"Charlotte died," Mary said bleakly. "Didn't you read about it in the newspaper?"

"I never bother to read them," Levanah said. "The estate takes up all my time. I administer it on Johnny's behalf. Johnny is my son. Did you know I married Teddy?"

"And he was killed. Yes, I know."

"Too terribly sad," Levanah said. "Johnny and Selena—I had twins—are eleven now. They're both away at school. And Cousin Wenna—"

"Married Cal. I read that too."

"And after poor Cal was killed, she actually caught herself another husband, and you will never guess who he is!"

"I think I heard the name somewhere."

"Michael Shaw, the artist. And do you know who Michael Shaw is? My father! My mother's lover was Michael Shaw, and he never even knew that I existed until I was eighteen years old. I visited him once very briefly when I was in London, and then I saw nothing of him until a few months after Teddy was killed when he turned up here and married Cousin Wenna. They live at Whittle Farm with the son she had by Cal. Michael is past eighty now, but he's absolutely marvelous!"

"My mother," said Mary. "Is my mother still here?"

"Aunt Leah is still at Kingsmead," Levanah said, sitting down without invitation. Over her shoulder she said, "Mary dear, I would adore a cup of coffee. Do go and make some for us while I gossip with your husband."

Mary went back into the kitchen, and Levanah's pale mouth curved into a smile as she bestowed her attention upon Franz.

"Do sit down," she said pleasantly. "I wonder if Mary has told you all about us."

"A little." He sat down, tension stiffening his spine.

"We were brought up together by my aunt," Levanah said. "Aunt Leah was always very fond of children. She had only the one girl before she was widowed, but Teddy's parents obligingly died and so did my mother, so that gave her three to mold and rear. She kept my father and me from knowing each other, and she drove Mary away by her possessiveness. But we came back, you see."

"Yes." He was fascinated by her eyes, more like those of a fox than a woman.

"I was sent away because Aunt Leah said I was a bad influence on Mary, but I came back and married Teddy. My father went away and came back more than a quarter of a century later. And now Mary has come home. Kingsmead draws us all back, you see."

She was smiling still, her fingers spread out like a fan. Franz was relieved when Mary returned with the laden tray. As she set it down she said apologetically, "I meant to write to you, Levanah."

"But you decided to surprise us instead. And I love surprises!" Levanah cried.

"My mother—"

"Will be delighted to see you. A pity you chose a German for your husband! There is still a certain amount of prejudice, but you were not, of course, in the Army?"

Her glance at his boot was delicate.

"We have a baby," Mary said defensively. "We have a daughter called Sigrid. She's asleep in the bedroom."

"A baby! How clever of you!" Levanah's eyes mocked. "And I have Johnny and Selena, and Wenna has Giles. Did you know that Wenna's mother, old Aunt Catrin, died?"

"She was very old, wasn't she?"

"Darling, she was ancient, practically a national monument. Did Mary tell you, Franz, that she was our great-grandmother's sister? None of us ever met her, for she spent all her life up in the wilds of Wales. She had a little farm there which is Wenna's now, but it's been rented out to some woman or other who nursed the old lady at the end. Wenna will be delighted to know that you're back in Marie Regina, Mary."

She went on chatting gaily, mentioning people of whom Franz had never heard, leaping lightly from one topic to another. She had set out to charm and Franz watched her with the same admiration as he would have watched a faultlessly executed stage performance.

She broke off abruptly as the rattle of wheels sounded from below. Mary had risen, apprehension in her pale face.

"It's Aunt Leah!" Levanah said. "She and Cousin Wenna both insist on using a buggy as if the old queen were still alive. Here she comes, Mary. Don't you find this a very emotional moment?"

Mary said nothing, but stood very still, her eyes fixed on the door. The woman who came in was clad, like Levanah, in black, a crepe veil covering her gray hair, a short-handled crop in her gloved hand.

"Aunt Leah, do see who Mrs. von Braun turns out to be!" cried Levanah.

The woman's heavy dark eyes flickered to Mary's face, and a long shudder ran through the gaunt frame. All she said, however, in a dully indifferent voice, was, "So you've come back."

"Mary is married to Franz von Braun, our new teacher," Levanah said. "It was a complete surprise, I promise you."

"What happened to Charlotte Bishop?" Leah asked.

"Charlie died. How are you, Mother?" Mary asked shrinkingly.

"Well enough. You know that Teddy was killed?"

"I've been bringing Mary up to date on all the family gossip," Levanah said.

"And I have a daughter," Mary said, nervously licking her lips. "Franz and I have a baby girl called Sigrid."

"Your first grandchild, Aunt Leah," said Levanah.

"I had not thought you capable of bearing children," Leah said stonily. "Let me see her."

Mary flustered out of the room. Leah, her eyes moving to Franz, said, "I was told the new teacher was a German. I do not approve of the German race."

"My mother was English," he found himself apologizing and stopped, annoyed with himself.

"I'm sure it's none of my concern," Leah said indifferently. "Is this the child?" She turned as Mary came back with Sigrid and took the baby into her own arms, staring down into the little face.

"She is not much like a Falcon," she said at last. "More like a German with that coloring."

"Wasn't Willow Falcon said to be very blond?" Levanah reminded her.

"So she was. Willow Falcon was one of those who bore the mark," Leah said to Franz. "She died in tragic circumstances as so many of our family have done. As she lay dying she said, 'Victory will not come until a Falcon rides upon a moth.' That was in my mother's time, but she often spoke of it."

"Does the babe have the mark?" Levanah asked.

"No! No, she doesn't," Mary said sharply.

"She's a pretty thing," Leah said. "I like babies. I like Falcon babies."

The two women in black encircled the child like two crows about a very small rabbit. Mary made a little stifled sound and took Sigrid back.

"Upon my word," Leah said, "but you act as if I were about to drop her."

"If you did so on this carpet," Levanah said thoughtfully, "not much damage would be done. If you dropped her at Kingsmead, in the hall say, her poor little skull would be smashed. People with smashed skulls bleed from the ears, don't they, Aunt Leah?"

"I believe so." Leah spoke flatly, her arms wrapped about her body as if she missed the warmth of the child.

"In this out-of-the-way place," Levanah said, "it's astonishing how many bits of information one manages to pick up. You will come over to Kingsmead, won't you? Mary, you'll want to show Franz over the house and grounds, won't you?"

"If Mother doesn't mind."

"Come if you wish," Leah said coolly. "It's not my house now."

"Nor mine," Levanah said sweetly. "I hold it in

trust for Johnny as Aunt Leah held it for Teddy. Just think, Mary, if you had married Teddy the estate would belong to your child now."

"And I would be a widow," Mary said with a flash of spirit.

"Poor Teddy was a hero," said Levanah. "Killed in action. That has a certain ring about it, don't you think?" Again her yellow eyes gleamed toward Franz's boot.

"There is no merit in slaughter," he said.

"I am glad we agree," Leah said. "Teddy's death was a cruel blow to me. I thought of him as my own boy. His being killed was a tragedy."

"For me also," said Levanah gently. "But I have consoled myself with the twins. You will like them both when you meet them, Franz. Johnny is full of life and mischief and Selena is his shadow, his adoring shadow."

"Wenna's boy is a fine boy too," Leah said.

"Giles is such a—country name," Levanah shrugged. "With such a name he couldn't be anything but a farmer!"

"Your child is not much like a Falcon," Leah said, "except for a certain something about the nose. What do you think, Levanah?"

"Oh, now that Mary is home again," Levanah said, smiling, "I'm sure that we can turn her baby into a real Falcon."

"Her name is Sigrid von Braun," Franz said coldly.

"But of course she is," Levanah said. "Only you must not grudge us a small share of her."

"I must change her," Mary said. Her voice was high and nervous, and the color came and went in her face.

"And we must leave. Aunt Leah, if you're going into the village you'd better order some sugar. I promised Johnny that I'd send him a cake. His last letter complained that at his school the boys are starved as a matter of policy!"

"He sounds like a very normal boy," Franz smiled.

"Oh, we are all very normal here," Levanah said. "You must not believe all the wild tales that have been handed down about us, Franz. And I shall look forward very much to seeing you at Kingsmead."

Her mouth curved upward again and she gave him a long, slanting look. As she went down the stairs he heard her begin to hum.

"I'll see to the baby." Mary hurried back into the bedroom.

"This must be a—shock for you, Mrs. Simmons," Franz said. "I feel I ought to have been honest, but Mary was afraid that there might be some opposition to her return."

"She left of her own free will against my wishes," Leah said. "She went away with that unnatural young woman, Charlotte Bishop. I disowned her then. Now she returns as your wife. I shall treat her with the courtesy due to your wife."

"I thought it best to bring her," Franz said.

"To lay the ghosts of childhood?" A bitter smile twisted her thin lips. "You are a fool," said Leah. "Don't you know that Kingsmead eats us all up, and that we cannot hope to return to a fire without being burned?"

She had gone before he could answer. A moment later the buggy retreated down the drive.

"It was not as bad as I feared," Mary said from the bedroom door. "My mother was not too angry."

"She hides her feelings very carefully," Franz said.

"Levanah has not changed at all," Mary commented. "She is calmer in her manner perhaps."

"She's a strange woman." He thought again of the yellow eyes, the curving mouth, the heavy scent of musk. He said abruptly, "I think I will go out for a while, just to stroll around. Will you be all right?"

"I'm going to unpack," Mary said. "Later I'll walk down into the village. It will be pleasant to get used to the place again. I will get used to it, but you must give me a little time."

"I'll help you later with the meal," Franz promised. For some reason he couldn't define, Mary, an apron round her waist and a soiled towel in her hand, made him feel restless and ill at ease.

Autumn had almost surrendered to winter and the wind was keen. Franz walked slowly down the curving drive toward the main road. He hoped it had not been a mistake to bring Mary back, but she had seemed anxious to return to her birthplace. As for his own feelings they were a curious medley of pleasure in the countryside and fear, though of what he could not tell.

A gentleman approaching him slowed his step as he came up and lifted his hat courteously.

"Mr. von Braun? My daughter met me on her way back to Kingsmead and told me that you had arrived. My wife and I hope to have the pleasure of calling on you as soon as you are more settled."

"That's very kind of you, Mr—?"

"Forgive me. Michael Shaw."

"Cousin Wenna's husband," said Franz, "and Lady Falcon's father."

He stopped, uncertain how to proceed, but the other smiled.

"I am eight-one years old and past the age of embarrassment," he said. "Levanah has now decided to acknowledge me as her father, and to forgive me for having loved her mother. She told me that your wife is Leah Simmons' daughter."

"Mary wished to come home to heal the breach with her mother."

"I am glad of it," said Michael. "I came back here myself to heal a breach. And I found a happiness that I believed I had lost."

"In your marriage."

"In my marriage," Michael said nodding. "I look forward to having you meet my wife. She is a very beautiful woman. Sometimes I think that if Levanah's mother had lived she would have become as Wenna is now. I am a most fortunate human being."

He looked, Franz thought, the epitome of contented and healthy old age. Thick white hair crowned his head above a high, tanned brow. His back was still straight and his eyes, set deeply under heavy lids, looked with twinkling humor at the younger man.

"You look—"

"Oh, don't say I look marvelous for my age," Michael said. "That remark is calculated to put years on me!"

"I was going to say that you look like a man who is completely fulfilled."

Michael Shaw laughed. "You express yourself well," he said.

"For a German?"

"Touché." Again that warm smile flashed in the lined brown face. "You may have to cope with some prejudice here, I'm afraid, but if you are yourself alone the villagers will respect you."

"I could not fight in the war even if I had

wished it." Glancing down at his foot, Franz said what he had never said to anyone. "I was born a cripple. When I was a boy I wore irons on my leg. When I grew up I decided that I would throw away the irons and limp a little."

"It is better to have scars one can see," Michael said, "than an inner corruption that cannot be admitted or cured."

"You are speaking of Lady Levanah," Franz said and stopped, appalled at his own tactlessness, but there was something about the other man that invited frankness.

"My daughter is not a happy woman," said Michael. "She has a great many responsibilities. The estate is a large one, and I'm afraid that her late husband squandered a great deal of money. She takes her duties most seriously and one has to admire her for that."

"And she has Mrs. Simmons' help."

"Yes." Michael hesitated and then said, "You will not take it amiss, I hope, if an old man offers you a word of advice? You are a newcomer here and you are married to a Falcon, to Leah Simmons' daughter. There is much about the family you may not know. There is, I suspect, much about themselves the family do not know. It would not do, I think, to allow either yourself or your wife to become too deeply involved in their affairs. My own wife and I maintain a friendly cordiality with those who live at Kingsmead, but we preserve our independence."

"And we may call at Whittle Farm?"

"Yes, indeed. Wenna and I will be delighted. You will enjoy meeting my stepson. Giles is a fine boy. We are very proud of him."

"I'll be happy to bring Mary over to see you," Franz said.

Michael's handshake was warm and firm. As he went slowly past he turned briefly to give a reassuring smile. Acknowledging it, Franz wondered why it was necessary for him to be reassured.

Chapter 8

"Four years have passed so quickly," said Levanah, stretching. "Who would have thought that we would have all settled down together so comfortably!"

Comfortable, thought Franz, was hardly the word that described her.

On this hot July afternoon she looked as cool as a black-winged butterfly, the wide sleeves of her narrow-skirted gown floating over her delicate wrists. Her hair, curving redly toward her jawbone, glinted in the sunlight. Under the thick golden lashes her amber eyes slanted lazily. Behind them both the two wings of Kingsmead reached out at each side of the rose garden, where blooms hung heavy on the carefully tended bushes. Before them the lawns stretched to the darkness of the woods.

Franz had never managed to sort out in his mind his conflicting emotions toward the house. Part of him appreciated the elegance of its structure, the beauty of its stone and ivied casements, yet another part of him shrank from the atmosphere of the place.

It had been intended, he felt, to be a happy, gracious building, but too many sad events had occurred there. Levanah had told him of some of them.

"They say Regina Falcon died on the stairs there when she was quite an old woman. She was mistress of Charles the Second, you know, and bore him a son, the 'wicked Lord Charles.' Handsome, isn't he?"

They had been on the gallery and she had nodded toward the portrait of the gentleman with black hair and eyes that stared coldly out of a proud face.

"It's said he had more private murders to his credit than any man in the country," Levanah had said. "He made a pact with the devil so his conscience was not troubled overmuch, but he was haunted by something all the same, for he gave orders that the family tomb was to be triple-locked, for fear, I suppose, that anyone should get out! He is quite my favorite ancestor."

"And this one?" He pointed to an early portrait, the girl's yellow eyes dreaming into space, red hair as lank as water dripping over green-swathed shoulders.

"That was the Lady Catrin. She was swum as a witch in the seventeenth century. One of the Welsh Falcons she was. And this one is Willow Falcon."

"The one who made the prophecy?"

" 'Victory will not come until a falcon rides upon a moth,' " she quoted.

He had looked for a long time at the round face with the pale hair and the downslanting gray eyes.

"She bore the witch mark too," said Levanah, watching him. "My mother had it and my grandmother and others before her, reaching back into the centuries. These days, of course, we don't believe in such things, do we?"

He had not answered and she had laughed softly, lips parting over the little, pointed teeth.

Now she said, from the depths of the wicker chair where she lounged, "A penny for them!"

"I was thinking that you are like Kingsmead," he said.

"How so?"

"Elegant and graceful, with a stillness at the heart."

"I am a widow." She gave him a long look. "I have no heart."

He was inclined to believe her. She was always sweetly pleasant but there was a coldness at the back of her eyes. It was not the emptiness of loss but something more subtle and more deadly.

"It's pleasant not to have any books to mark," he said abruptly.

Her eyes glinted with amusement but she accepted the change of subject.

"You have proved an excellent teacher," she said warmly. "I hear nothing but praise for you in the village and the folk of Marie Regina are slow to accept strangers. We will have to think about getting you an assistant one day if the number of pupils continues to increase."

"We will be losing one very soon," he reminded her.

"When Giles goes to agricultural college?" She made a little impatient gesture. "I cannot understand why Wenna insisted on giving her son private tuition instead of his going either to Maidstone Grammar School or to boarding school. She is sadly possessive!"

"Giles himself refused to leave the farm."

"And how can a boy of seventeen possibly decide what is good for him!" she exclaimed.

"He is an intelligent student."

"With nothing in his head but tractors and hay-making. Well, it will do him good to get away from home, and not be tied to his mother's apron strings," Levanah said.

"Selena will be staying at home now, I take it?"

Levanah cast him a sharp look, but said calmly, "Too much attention is not a good idea for a girl. It spoils her marriage prospects. Johnny, of course, will go up to Oxford eventually, and then take his seat in the Lords. I hope he will develop a greater sense of responsibility, but there is a great deal of his father in him. Teddy was forever dreaming up some wild-cat scheme or other, and the only certain result was that sooner or later the estate would lose money by it!"

"Your aunt thought a great deal of him, I understand."

"Meaning that I did not? I married him, you know."

"Yes."

"He and Wenna's husband were killed on the same day. Nine years ago." Levanah said. "Time goes so quickly. I shall be thirty-seven next year."

"You don't look it," he said truthfully.

There was not a line on her pale skin and her shape under the tube dress was as hard and taut as that of a young girl.

"Mary and I are the same age," she said softly.

Mary's delicate prettiness was blurring a little and there were gray streaks in her hair.

"Dear Mary!" Levanah thrust out a silk-clad leg and contemplated it idly. "How charming it is to see her and Aunt Leah reconciled! And we are all devoted to little Sigrid."

A slight frown crumpled his brow. Four-year-old Sigrid was the darling of his heart, so it was surely natural for her relatives to love her too, but he could never see her in the company of Leah or Levanah without feeling a cold clutch of fear.

"Mary has not been well," he said.

"I thought she was looking a little peaked. She was always inclined to be a little nervy, you know. She's seen the doctor?"

"She is expecting another child," Franz confided.

"Another baby at Kingsmead! Oh, but this is delightful," Levanah said gaily. "When will it be born?"

"At Christmas, we think."

"'Unto us a child is born,'" quoted Levanah. "Are you both pleased about it?"

"Very pleased," he said, but the frown lingered. Mary had not been herself for weeks. She had carried Sigrid with ease, but this child was taking its toll of her in constant sickness and sleepness nights.

"Here they come now," Levanah said, glancing back toward the French windows.

Leah, her black dress still unfashionably long, said as she and her daughter approached, "Mary has been telling me—"

"About the new baby? Franz just told me. Isn't it splendid! Do you want another girl? Girls are such good companions."

"Mary has not been well," Leah said in her flat voice. "She is constantly sick and tired."

"Sigrid must require so much attention," said Levanah. "I remember what Selena was like at that age! And doing your own housework and cooking too, Mary! Franz, you ought not to allow it."

"I like to do my own work," Mary protested.

"Surely we pay you enough to employ at least a daily help!" Levanah said to Franz.

"Mary dislikes having people about the flat," Franz said stiffly.

"Lord! but we would be in a pickle if we dismissed all the servants at Kingsmead!" Levanah said gaily. "The simple life is all very fine, my dear cousin, but you must think of yourself now and of the child. Tell her, Franz, that she must take things more easily."

"I do get tired," Mary confessed.

"And Franz will soon be busy with the school again," said Levanah. "Well, if you won't have a maid—why, Aunt Leah, wouldn't it be a good idea if we took care of little Sigrid until the baby is born? Mary, you'd let her come to Kingsmead, wouldn't you?"

"Well, I—I don't know." Mary looked hesitatingly at Franz, but Levanah went on.

"Sigrid loves Kingsmead as much as she loves her own home. We could fix up one of the bedrooms as a nursery for her. And I'd bring her over to the Manor School every day. You wouldn't object to that, would you, Franz, for Mary's sake?"

"No, of course not," he said.

"Then it's settled! Aunt Leah, you will help me to care for Sigrid, I know. You were always so devoted to little ones. There is no sacrifice you wouldn't make for a child, is there?" Levanah said.

Her eyes and mouth were gentle and amused. Leah's own dark eyes shifted and fell before her niece's amber gaze.

"We would love to have Sigrid," was all she said.

"Of course, if you thought it best, Mary could come back to Kingsmead as well until after the child is born," Levanah said.

"My place is with Franz," Mary said. Imperceptibly she had moved closer to him.

"How sweet to see such devotion," Levanah said. "It would be very wrong of us to try to dissuade you."

"I'll have the room next to Selena's made into a nursery," Leah said.

"Mary and I used to sleep in those two rooms, over the servants' quarters," Levanah mused. "Do you remember, Mary? Selena has one room now and the other is a guest room, but it is so seldom in use that it will be perfect for Sigrid."

"I'll come back with you now in the buggy to gather her things together," Leah said. "She will stay without fretting, I'm sure."

"Where is Sigrid?" Franz asked.

"In the kitchen, stuffing herself with cake," Mary said.

"Best leave her then. Shall we go over to the Manor School?"

Leah held out her hand to her daughter with an air of resignation rather than affection.

"And Franz and I will make shift to amuse ourselves while you are gone," Levanah said. "You'll be coming back here to collect Franz like a good dutiful wife, won't you, Mary?"

"Shall I drive you both over?" Franz offered.

"And leave me alone? How ungallant of you!" Levanah said lightly. "Mary, scold your husband heartily for me."

"Mother and I can manage," Mary said.

"There, you see! You would only be in the way. Come up and see the room we plan to give Sigrid while she is staying with us!"

Her fingers bit into his arm and her smile coaxed. He allowed himself to be led away.

As he followed Levanah through the long drawing room into the hall, Sigrid's chatter issued from the direction of the kitchen. He hesitated but his hostess was urging him toward the stairs.

"The room was redecorated in pink only two years ago," she said. "You remember the trouble I had with those dreadful men who tried to overcharge me because I was the mother of a lord? I was not happy about the shade either. Redheads should not, in my opinion, be seen against pink, but Selena assures me that disharmony is all the rage. Now, do you think darling Sigrid will be happy here?"

She had opened the door of the pink-painted room and waved her arm within.

"We will leave her door and the one into the main gallery open and a light burning, in case she needs anything during the night," she went on. "Selena has the room next door and will go to her at once. And we will clear a shelf for her dolls."

"It's very kind of you," he said uncomfortably.

"Mary will be much more rested," Levanah said, "and we will enjoy spoiling Sigrid a little. It will be marvelous to have a child in the house again, and Selena will be happy. She's very fond of Sigrid."

"And of Giles too?"

He was pleased to see a flash of what might have been anger disturb the sweetness of her expression. She shrugged, however, and said calmly, "A boy and girl infatuation! At fifteen girls are apt to succumb to romantic fancies. Fortunately the whole thing will die a natural death when Giles goes away to college."

"You know exactly what you want for your family, don't you?" he said.

"I think I know what is best for them," Levanah said coolly, "but there are things I want for myself too. I shall get them—in time."

Her eyes, resting upon him, were sleepy. Unwillingly he took a step closer and the warmth of musk stirred his senses.

From below a voice called. "Mother! Mother, are you upstairs?"

"Up here, darling!" Levanah glided back into the gallery.

Selena, dark red curls held in place by a bandeau, ran up the stairs. She looked flushed and pretty, her short pleated skirt whipping about her slim legs. She talked, as she mounted toward them, in a series of breathless gasps.

"Aunt Mary says Sigrid is coming. Can she stay in my room? And may I go to the dance at Maidstone on Saturday? Giles says he will take me in the buggy. It's not a late affair and I'll be back in plenty of time for—hello, Uncle Franz."

"Sigrid will be visiting here for a while. She will be sleeping in the room next to yours. You may not go to the dance."

"Oh, Mother, why not?" Selena protested.

"Because you are too young to attend public functions unchaperoned," Levanah said.

"Oh, stuff! Nobody bothers about chaperones in this day and age," the girl exclaimed.

"I bother!" her mother said coldly. "When you are eighteen you will be presented and have your London season. Until then I will not have you running all over the county with every young man that takes your fancy."

"Giles is a relative!" Selena said hotly.

"Giles is the son of my cousin, and on the fringe of the family," Levanah said.

"You never liked him! You never have a good word to say for him." Tears sparkled in the indignant gray eyes.

"Giles is a most personable young man," Levanah returned serenely, "and it is greatly to his credit that he takes his duties on the farm so seriously. But I will not allow you to attend a public dance with him or with anybody else. So you may remove that scowl from your face, young lady, and if you intend flouncing into your room, refrain from slamming the door. Slammed doors are a sign of ill breeding."

Her cheeks flaming as redly as her hair, Selena went haughtily into her room, closing the door behind her with ostentatious care.

"She is disappointed," Franz said.

"But I could not have been expected to give permission, surely?"

"No, no, of course not." He gave a final sympathetic glance over his shoulder. "You had to be firm."

"She is planning to sneak out anyway," Levanah said wryly, taking his arm as they began to descend the stairs. "I know my dear daughter and when she refrains from arguing that means she intends to disobey."

"What will you do?" he asked curiously.

"Well, I can scarcely lock her in her room on bread and water in this day and age," Levanah said. "We will just have to hope that something turns up."

She smiled as she spoke and made a curious little gesture with her left hand. For a moment Franz had the impression that the black pearl on her forefinger glowed with a life of its own.

"Come and talk to your own daughter," she invited. "You will want to tell her she's going to stay here for a while."

It was Levanah, however, who went ahead of him into the big kitchen and scooped up the small blond child, who raised a sugar-sticky mouth for a kiss.

"Sigrid, would you like to stay with us for a while?" she asked.

"With Mother and Father?" Sigrid asked.

"By yourself, like a grown-up girl," Levanah said.

"With Dolly?"

"With all your dolls. You can sleep in the pink bedroom, next to Selena. You'd like that, wouldn't you?"

Sigrid considered the question carefully and then nodded.

"I like Selena," she said gravely, "but not Johnny. Johnny pulled my hair."

"Johnny will be going back to school soon, and while he's at home I promise he won't pull your hair."

"Then I'll stay." Unlike most children Sigrid never wriggled to be put down, but waited patiently until she was set on her feet, when she trotted to the other end of the kitchen to have her face sponged by Cook.

"This is a nice room," Franz said, looking appreciatively at the scrubbed wooden surfaces, the copper pans hanging against the whitewashed wall. "In Germany, when I was a boy, we had such a kitchen there. Smaller than this, but warm and friendly. This room is very old but it is happy."

"Probably because tragedy and breadmaking don't

go together. All the dramas in the family went on in other parts of the house, and servants were not really expected to have private lives."

Sigrid, face damp and shiny, ran back to Levanah. "Am I cleaned up?" she demanded.

"Beautifully cleaned up—what on earth is that noise?" The heavy tramping of feet in the side yard mingled with voices raised in excited commiseration. Cook, at a nod from her mistress, pulled open the heavy door to admit four farm laborers, two of whom supported a white-faced Giles.

"Sorry, Cousin Levanah, but I took a tumble from Bess at the end of your drive," he said wincingly as he was lowered to a chair.

"Never knew that mare to turn skittish before," one of the men said.

"Was it a rabbit?" Levanah knelt to examine the boy's rapidly swelling ankle.

"It wasn't anything," Giles said. "One minute I was riding along minding my own business and the next Bess reared up as if she'd seen the devil, and over I went. *Ow!*"

"Your ankle is badly sprained, but I don't think any bones are broken," Levanah said. "I'll strap it up for you and get out the car to run you to the doctor. Was the horse hurt?"

"She galloped home without stopping to find out what had happened to me," Giles said ruefully.

"One of you had better get over to Whittle Farm or Cousin Wenna will be in a panic," Levanah said. "I really must see about having a telephone installed here. All this running about whenever anything happens is positively medieval! Mary and Mother should be back soon with Sigrid's things. Cook, get me some bandage from the medicine chest, and a knife. This boot will have to be cut off."

She was all practical efficiency, rolling back her sleeves, shoving the men out of the kitchen, sitting the child up on the table out of harm's way. Her voice, light and clear, ran on soothingly.

Franz went out into the great hall again and stood still, fighting down irrational panic. From the gallery above Selena called down,

"What is it, Uncle Franz? What's all the noise about?"

"Giles took a toss and sprained his ankle."

"Oh, no! Poor Giles! But surely not from Bess? Bess is so docile."

"She was frightened by something."

"And now Giles won't be able to go to the dance even if I can talk Mother round," Selena said in exasperation.

"She would not have allowed you to attend, and you *are* very young," Franz said.

"She never wants me to go anywhere," Selena said resentfully. "I was never allowed to invite any girl friends here in the holidays either. Once I swore I'd tell them that we never have guests because Aunt Leah was peculiar and went about telling people she was the Empress Josephine, and then Mother said that Alexa Smythe Jones could come and spend Easter with us. I was fearfully excited because Alexa was quite my bosom friend at that time and we made all kinds of plans, and then in the end it all came to nothing because Alexa got scarlet fever and was in quarantine for centuries! I must go and see how Giles is. Honestly! What rotten luck!"

"Selena!" Franz put out a detaining hand.

"Yes, Uncle Franz?" Gray eyes looked at him inquiringly.

"It is nothing—only that I hope you will take good care of Sigrid while she is visiting here. You will, won't you?"

"Yes, of course." Selena looked puzzled.

"I worry about her."

"She'll be as right as rain at Kingsmead," she assured him. "Mother thinks the world of Sigrid, and you know how Aunt Leah is with children! I must go to Giles."

The door swung open and shut behind her. The hall dimmed as if her going took a brightness from it. Franz walked slowly to the front door, where light fell in squares of gold on the stone floor. At each side of him the ancient tapestries stirred. Looking at them he thought that once they must have been gay with bright colors. Now, in the tarnished gold of a lady's headdress, the streak of rusted crimson on a knight's cloak, the vibrant life of the past sought to return amid folds of muffling and sinister gray.

He stared at the faded embroideries, wondering what would happen if they could speak. Would the stiff-limbed figures tell of past evil they had seen enacted in this house, or would they warn of present danger?

Chapter 9

Cat, staring into the flames of the fire, said, "Leone! I'm going to have a seeing time!"

"This minute? Can't it wait until the turkey is stuffed?"

The older woman looked up from her task but received no reply. Her companion sat, with folded hands and bent black head, her eyes slitted upon the glowing wood.

"Wait then, and I'll join you." Leone wiped her hands hastily, seized pad and pencil and sat down in the rocking chair.

"Describe what you see," she said crisply.

"The big house again," Cat said. "I see a room in the big house."

"What type of room?"

"Bedroom, I think. A woman in the bed and two women with her. They are helping her to—ah, now I see more clearly! She is having a baby."

"Can you see the faces?"

"Too dim. They bend over the bed. The woman on the bed is moaning."

Cat put her hands to her stomach and began to whimper.

"Report what you see, and don't begin to identify with it," Leone commanded.

"Things are not going well," Cat said. "The woman has been in labor for a long time and she is growing weaker. Her baby is going to be born in a moment. That's odd!"

"What is?"

"One of the women helping has put out her left hand. There is a black ring on her forefinger, but it glows. Black but glowing."

"What else can you see?"

"Nothing, nothing at all. The whole scene is fading," Cat said in a disappointed tone, shaking her head slightly.

"I'll get you a sandwich," Leone said. "A nice ham sandwich. It's a marvelous way of filling the stomach and anchoring the mind."

"Did it make any sense?" Cat asked. "It was very clear, very sharp."

"It would make sense if we could see the whole picture," Leone said, cutting ham into thin, succulent slices. "But it must have been important, I think."

"To me? I didn't know the people."

"To you, or to the babe that's being born."

"I wish I could have seen more." Cat accepted the sandwich and munched thoughtfully.

"We will send out a loving thought to the new baby," Leone said, folding her hands briefly and bowing her head. The oil lamp suspended on its hook from the ceiling cast a warm glow over her coiled blond hair.

"Poor thing, to be born on Christmas Eve and only get one present," Cat said pityingly.

"Mercenary Mary!" Leone teased, returning to the half-filled turkey.

"I wish I knew for certain how much of what I see is true," Cat said restlessly. "And what use is it to me or anybody else anyway?"

"I can't answer that," Leone said. "I can only tell you these seeing times come to you for a purpose. Perhaps you are being led."

"The great house is Kingsmead where my mother lives, I'm sure of it," Cat said. "I wish I could go there, Leone. I wish I could find out the sort of person she is."

"When the time is ripe you'll know it," Leone said placidly. "Shall we trim the tree now? The bird's done, and Lord help us! from the size of it we'll still be eating the wretched thing at Easter!"

"I'll get the tinsel," Cat said, jumping up and hurrying into the bedroom.

Leone sighed as she began to peel potatoes. Cat would be eighteen in March, and her nature was too restless and inquiring to be content with a placid existence on the tiny farm. In the two years since she had left school she had grown into a beauty, her legs long and slim under her short skirt, her eyes emerald in a heart-shaped face, her hair a waterfall of blackness. Sooner or later the lads would come courting and Leone was afraid that her impulsive charge would rush into marriage and tire of it. Better for her to seek fresh horizons for a time, then later, if she chose, she could come back and settle down with a local boy. Yet Leone was unwilling to part with the girl. Cat was too vulnerable, too eager to rush into affairs that she was too inexperienced to handle properly.

"I've found those acorns we gilded last year," Cat said, coming out of the bedroom with the tree decorations in her hands.

"We'll put them on the tree, and I'll make a big pot of stew for any who come in need."

"Times are hard," Cat said solemnly.

"Little you and I know about it," Leone chided. "We have plenty to eat and my money pays the rent, so we've no cause to grumble, but they say times are bad right enough, with too many chasing too few jobs, and a little bunch of people at the top spending all the money."

"I suppose the Falcons are very rich?" Cat said.

"I suppose so." Slicing the potatoes thickly into the pot, Leone frowned slightly. Having heard something of Cat's beginnings from the old woman she had made it her business to try to find out more about the girl's relatives, but information was scanty.

As far as Leone could gather the Falcons were an old established Kentish family whose estates totaled a comfortable thousand acres. A hereditary peerage had been granted to them at the time of the Restoration and they had lived, generation after generation, in the same village. From time to time the usual kind of scandals cropped up, but there were, as old Aunt Catrin had related, hints of darker tragedies, of women with the crescent moon on their thighs who could both see and shape the future.

In recent years according to the scanty hints in back copies of various newspapers over which Leone had pored at the library, the Falcon family had lived blameless lives. Lady Levanah, widow of Lord Edward Falcon, was administering the estate on behalf of her son, Lord John. Her maternal aunt, Leah Simmons, and her daughter Selena lived with her. Nothing there to explain Cat's intense fragments of vision. But the black ring on the left forefinger in the latest seeing time corresponded with old Aunt Catrin's rambles.

"Queer she was with that red hair and those yellow eyes, more like a fox than a woman. And a black pearl on her hand. She used to sit close to the fire staring at the black stone and then she would laugh, not sweet and loving, but mocking and low, like an echo of herself. Took no interest in the baby at all, only told me to put it in the orphanage and left the moonstone ring to pay for it."

And the crystal, the wooden figure and the picture of her own mother, Leone thought. She wondered what they had represented to the strange, secret girl, or had they been parts of her life that she had cast aside as she cast aside her unwanted child?

Abruptly Leone said, "This seeing power you have was given to you for some reason. I've tried to show you how to control and develop it, but there are other things for you to learn if you choose. I can teach you how to draw down power and use that power to help people, to set things right. I can teach you to protect yourself against the evil that others intend you."

"To set what things right?" Cat asked.

"I'm not sure yet," Leone said slowly. "I can only tell you there is some kind of pattern in all this. I am part of it but I'm not certain why. That first day I met you there was a bond between us."

"And Kingsmead, the big house, is that part of it too?"

"I think so, but not yet. We must wait."

"And learn all those things you spoke about?" Cat said eagerly.

"You'll be eighteen soon," said Leone. "Think about it, and if you're still of the same mind then, I'll do what I can. I was trained myself years ago by a very wise man, but it was hard for me, not being gifted with the seeing, and I've not used my knowledge for a long time."

"I'll leap ahead," Cat said cheerfully.

"And fall flat on your face many times, I've no doubt," Leone said wryly.

"When we had the drought last summer," Cat said slowly, "our well never ran dry. Did you do that, Leone? Will you show me how to do it? I'm sure that I could create positive floods if I set my mind to it."

"I've no doubt you could," Leone agreed. "How about creating a few positive scrubbed carrots to add to this stew?"

"Tonight," said Cat loftily, "I have a soul about carrots! Leone, who is Margot?"

"Margot? I've no idea. Why?" Leone reached for the onions.

"I don't know." Cat looked puzzled. "The name just came into my head, that's all."

She shrugged, putting down the gilded acorns, and went to join Leone.

"Margot," Franz was saying, "was my grandmother's name. We had decided, if the child was a girl—"

"It's a very pretty name," Levanah said. "I like it very much. Don't you, Aunt Leah?"

"We haven't had a Margot in the family before," Leah said.

"Such a pretty baby too, so brown and bonny," said Levanah. "We all adore her almost as much as we adore Sigrid."

"Sigrid has been so good," said Leah. "She asked where her mother was, and I explained that she had gone to heaven, and the little pet said at once, 'Then I will be the new baby's mother'!"

"She was only thirty-six years old," Franz said. "That is too young to die. Too young!"

"You must give yourself a little time," Levanah said. "It is only a week since poor Mary died."

"I ought to have insisted on her having a doctor," Franz said. "She was not well for months. I ought to have insisted."

"Nobody could have foreseen," said Levanah. "As a rule, if a woman carries badly she has an easy delivery. Mary was—unfortunate, that's all. I promise you that we did everything we could."

"I know. I'm very grateful," he said dully.

"We have to think of the future," Levanah said, sitting in the wing-backed chair opposite him. Against its creamy covers her glowing hair and severely cut black velvet dress showed to striking advantage.

"I can't think of anything," Franz said. "I can't settle to making plans."

"That's quite natural. You're still very shocked," Levanah said. "But you have two daughters to consider. You must think of Sigrid and Margot. They have no mother."

"Wenna has offered to look after them."

"Wenna? How very sweet of her, and how very impractical. She couldn't possibly take care of two young children, of course."

"She's a very efficient woman," Franz began.

"On the verge of sixty with a husband in his mid-eighties! Oh, I grant you that my father is really marvelous for his age, but he can't possibly look forward to having his nights disturbed by a crying baby. And when Giles comes home in the vacations he'll be wanting to study. How can he do that with Sigrid running around and demanding attention?"

"Sigrid is used to living here now," Leah said in her flat voice. "It would be very unwise to uproot her at this stage."

"It's not as if you'll never see them," Levanah said. "Sigrid will be coming over to school very soon and you'll be teaching her yourself. And naturally either Aunt Leah or I will bring Margot over every day."

They were talking sensibly, their expressions kindly and concerned, but he could only think of Mary as he had last seen her with a dreadful grayness like a film over her face and her hands crossed.

"Let them stay with us for the time being," Levanah said. "It will take you all your energy to adjust to being alone. And there is the school, the spring term due to begin."

"As you please." He spoke indifferently, the image of Mary still in his mind. "It's very kind of you, very kind of you both," he added belatedly.

"They are Falcon children," said Leah.

"Half von Braun children too," said Levanah playfully. "We must not deny the father's part."

"Will you stay over at Kingsmead for a few days longer?" Leah asked.

"No. Thank you but no. I will drive back to the flat tonight."

He had brought the car as a surprise for Mary, but she had never ridden in it.

"I'll come over tomorrow and sort through Mary's things for you," Levanah said.

"No. No, I would prefer to do it alone."

He could not endure the thought of those thin fingers rummaging among Mary's clothes.

"As you please." She rose in one graceful, fluid movement and held out her hand. "But you will come over as often as you possibly can?"

"Yes, of course." He bowed jerkily and made his escape. The word "escape" came into his mind as he went, and not until he was in the new car, steering it carefully down the winding drive, did he feel free to breathe easily again.

"I think," Wenna was saying as she prepared for bed, "that I will offer to sort out Mary's things. Would it be tactless of me?'

Michael, already in bed, propped himself on one elbow and considered.

"It would be very kind," he decided.

"I wonder if he will let us take care of the little girls," she mused.

"I doubt if Leah or Levanah will allow them to leave Kingsmead."

"I always wanted a daughter," Wenna said. "I envy Levanah her Selena. I even envied poor Mary. The new baby is so sweet. Well, I've got Giles, and he's a fine boy."

"Giles and I had a talk this afternoon," said Michael. "I asked him how he felt about being adopted legally by me."

"You never mentioned it!"

"I've thought about it these past few years," he told her. "I kept putting it off. All my life I've put things off, you know."

"I had noticed." She gave him a dry, affectionate glance over her shoulder.

"It would mean his changing his surname to 'Shaw,'" Michael said. "He doesn't mind, but we both wondered how you felt about it."

"I loved Cal," Wenna said slowly, "I loved him very much, but he's been gone for nearly ten years. You know it's only when I look at Giles that I remember Cal's face. He's very like him, but he has something of you in him too. Odd gestures, tricks of speech that he's picked up from you over the years. He's as much your son as Cal's now, and Giles Shaw is a good name."

"I'll have the papers drawn up," Michael said. "Are you coming to bed or are you going to sit gazing at yourself all night?"

"I was wondering if I ought to have my hair shingled," Wenna said, picking up a long strand of the silvery gray mass and squinting at it critically. "I am sadly out of fashion."

"Leave it be. Your hair is perfect."

"My eyebrows are too heavy," she complained, "and the lines on my face are getting deeper. And I've lost all my back teeth!"

"You're a crumbling ruin," he agreed.

"Am I?" She came over and slid into bed beside him, her green eyes teasing though there was a hint of wistfulness in her voice. "Am I getting old, Michael?"

"Beautifully so, like rare wine," he told her.

"Michael, I think the world of you!" she exclaimed. "These past years have been so happy for me."

"For me too." He put his arm around her, enjoying the warm curve of her breasts as she curled toward him. "For me too, girl."

"Do you want me?" she whispered.

They still made love now and then, twined together in the big bed, lamplight gilding gray hair, passion flaring briefly out of their deep affection.

"Later perhaps. Stay close," he returned.

She settled her head on his shoulder, feeling the steady beating of his heart under her hand. She woke sometimes in the night and reached out to feel that beating. He was wonderful for his age, but her love was shot through with an unadmitted fear.

It was strange, she reflected how her life had worked out. As a child on Saron Farm she had often heard her mother talk about her niece Margred who had gone into Kent to marry a Falcon cousin. She had thought of the Falcons as very rich and grand, and never imagined she would ever meet any of them. Then her young husband had been killed in the quarry and, when she had heard that Leah was looking for a teacher for the Manor School, she had been glad to leave her grief behind and travel to Marie Regina. She had been scarcely twenty, her brown hair coiled up, her green eyes friendly. For twenty years she had taught at the school that Leah had founded in memory of her mother, Lady Margred. It had been a queer, quiet life with herself always on the fringe of the family. She had seen much of what went on at Kingsmead, had helped to bring Levanah into the world, had wept over Beth's suicide, and after twenty years she had married Edith Falcon's bastard son, Cal, and borne him a son.

And after Cal's death Michael Shaw had come, and the man whom she had met briefly as Beth's friend nearly thirty years before had become her third husband.

"Are you asleep?" she whispered.

"Yes," Michael returned.

"I was thinking how odd life is," she said. "Some people have everything happen to them when they're young, but I had to wait until I was past forty before I began to live."

"Do you regret it?" he asked.

"I appreciate it," she said, putting her arms around his neck. "I appreciate it very much. I appreciate *you* very much, and Giles, and the farm. There's only one thing I regret."

"What's that, my love?"

"I wish I'd gone home to see Mam just once," she said wistfully. "I sent her money over the years, but I never went back to see her, and I could never persuade her to come to England. I cut myself off completely from my childhood and girlhood."

"We could go up to Wales next summer if you like," Michael said. "We could see the farm and meet the lady who's renting it. I can't recall her name."

"Leone Starbeck. She was there when Mam died. Don't you recall we had a letter from her, telling us how peaceful it had been?"

"So we did. A very pleasant, sympathetic letter. She has not written since."

"She sends the year's rent with a card at Christmas, nothing more. I hope she has kept the farm in good repair," Wenna fretted.

"My love, when you begin talking about your old home, it's a sure sign that something is worrying you," Michael said, abandoning his attempt to doze.

"Is it Giles? He seems very happy at the agricultural college."

"I was thinking about Levanah," Wenna said reluctantly. "Darling, I know she's your daughter, but after all you had no hand in her upbringing. She is Leah's handiwork."

"It was good of Leah to bring her up."

"You're so forgiving!" Wenna said in exasperation. "It was Leah who kept you and Beth apart and prevented your marriage. It was Leah who kept you and your daughter ignorant of each other's existence."

"You're starting to lose your temper," he warned teasingly.

"One day I will," she threatened, "but we were talking about Levanah."

"What about her?"

"I don't know," Wenna said slowly. "That's the trouble, Michael. I *don't know!* I was there when she was born; I taught her when she was little; I watched her grow up. I loved her for Beth's sake and I loved her for her own too. She was such a solemn little thing, always tagging after Mary and Teddy. I pitied her, I suppose. But I never really knew her at all. You know, don't you, that Leah discovered she was holding weird rituals down in the cottage. Oh, it was no more than childish nonsense, but Leah was very angry. Levanah was sent away for a long time."

"That was when she came to see me," Michael remembered. "A stiff little figure with a straw hat on her head. Very much on her dignity."

"She came back, and she was—not changed, but more herself," Wenna said. "It was as if she'd always been cool and still and mocking, and we'd never really noticed. She'd spent about six months with Mam up in Wales. I don't know why she took

it into her head to go there at all, but then I don't
know anything about her. She came back and married
Teddy and had the twins and was widowed, and has
lived quietly at Kingsmead, and I still don't know
anything about her at all. She and Leah hate each
other under all their politeness. I can feel them
hating each other. And now Sigrid and the new
baby are to be brought up at Kingsmead. And that
frightens me. I don't know why it should frighten
me, but it does. Michael, are you awake?"

His deep heavy breathing was her only answer.
She looked at him hopefully and he rolled away from
her, burying his face in the pillow, relaxing more
deeply into sleep. Later, sometime during the night,
he would turn to her again and she would wake in
his arms.

Perhaps it was best that he had fallen asleep.
Worry was dangerous for the elderly, and she spared
him anxiety whenever she could. Only sometimes
did her half-expressed fears rise to the surface and
bubble out. Afterward she always felt small and
selfish.

Now, curled against her husband's back, she began
to pray silently, her lips moving.

"Dear Lord, keep Michael safe for many years to
come, and help Giles to get through his first-year ex-
aminations with credit, and let the spring harvest be
a profitable one."

The moon, shining through a crack in the curtains, beat against her closed eyelids. She thrust her
face between Michael's shoulder blades and willed
sleep to come, but her lips still moved silently.

"Dear Lord, guard Sigrid and the new baby. Protect them. Protect them from Levanah."

Chapter 10

"But you cannot mourn for the rest of your life," Levanah said gently. "Mary would not have wished it. We were very close at one time and I know how she felt about things."

"I have no need to marry again," Franz said stubbornly, "I can take very good care of myself."

"No need, I agree; you're a most competent man. But what of desire?" She glanced at him and smiled to see the embarrassed flush in his thin face.

"I scarcely think" he began.

"That's my business? My dear cousin-in-law, this is 1930, not the Middle Ages. Women are aware that men have desires, and you are not an old man."

"I'm past forty-five," he said, "and was never accounted a Don Juan at any time."

"But Mary has been dead for nearly five years. You ought to think of marrying again."

She sounded sweetly concerned, her eyes gentle, veiled by the long golden lashes. Her hair was the same clear, light red it had been when she was a

child, though whether by nature or art he was not so-
phisticated enough to tell. Her gown of black chiffon softened her thin figure and she had tinted her
lips and nails a brownish coral. Her presence disturbed him as it always did, arousing in him a mixture of fascination and repulsion.

"There was a young lady once, in Germany," he
said slowly. "Oh, it was no more than a boy-and-girl
romance but it had a certain sweetness. I have not
heard of her for years, but it is possible she has neither moved nor married."

"You think she may have waited for you? How
very sentimental you are!"

"Perhaps I will take a trip to Germany," he said
thoughtfully. "It would do no harm. I could not
love another woman as I loved Mary, but a man
needs companionship, and I have not forgotten I
have two daughters to consider."

"Oh?" she raised her brows slightly.

"I can never thank you and Leah sufficiently for
your kindness to them," he said earnestly. "Both
Sigrid and Margot have much for which to be grateful, but you are right to urge me to marry again. It
is my duty to provide them with a mother."

"Is it necessary for you to go all the way to Germany for that?" she asked.

"I would like to spend a little time at home," he
said.

"So Germany is home? I was under the impression that you had been naturalized," she mocked.

"I didn't mean to sound ungrateful." His thin
face colored again.

"I was teasing you," said Levanah. Nobody
would have guessed, so sweet was her smile, that she
was coldly and bitterly angry. "It's natural you

should wish to go back to your father's land though I fear it will be greatly changed from when you were a boy. But to go all that way for a wife—"

"It was a passing thought," he said.

"You would do better to choose a wife from—nearer at hand."

Franz felt the stirrings of alarm. For years he had denied to himself the possibility that Levanah might be interested in him. He had assured himself that she was immersed in her children and in the management of the estate, that her manner toward him was no more than friendly, but as she leaned back on the sofa in a pose that was frankly inviting he was unable to deceive himself.

"I am not what is termed 'a good catch,'" he evaded. "I have nothing to offer beyond my teaching salary."

"Then you should marry a rich woman," she said archly.

"I would prefer a sensible young woman who can cook and sew and is fond of children," he said.

"What a perfect description of a typical hausfrau!" she exclaimed, laughing. "I wish you joy in your seeking. Ah, Sigrid! Come and say good afternoon to your father, and you come too, Margot! You ought not to be shy."

Thus admonished, his daughters came reluctantly in. As usual his heart leapt with pride and his nerves quivered with suppressed irritation. They were pretty children, Sigrid being pale and blond, Margot brown and rosy. He taught Sigrid every day and knew her to be intelligent. Margot, who was not yet five, still learned her alphabet at Leah's knee. But he came over to Kingsmead two or three times a week to see the younger child. There was no need for them to shuffle from one foot to the other, holding hands tightly and glancing toward Levanah as they chorused obediently, "Good afternoon, Father."

"Come and talk to me," he invited, and they came sedately down the long drawing room.

"Selena will be home next week," Levanah said brightly, "and she is going to take them for a picnic."

"How is Selena?" He reached out to take Margot on his knee, but the little girl stepped aside.

"Selena," said Levanah, allowing a little of her pent-up anger to escape, "is beyond my understanding! You know what a splendid season I gave her last year. She had some of the loveliest dresses any girl could have had, and it cost me a small fortune to rent a Mayfair house. She received four offers of marriage, two of them from the most highly connected gentlemen, and she turned them down flat. Can you imagine such stupidity! Now she either sulks in her room declaring I am a cruel, harsh woman for not allowing her to marry Giles, or she is off with those friends of hers, dancing until all hours, ruining her complexion with cigarettes."

"She is young yet," said Franz.

"Young and obstinate," Levanah said. "Girls, have you nothing at all to say to your father? He has driven over specially to see you."

"We said 'good afternoon,'" Sigrid said reproachfully.

"We said 'good afternoon, Father,'" corrected Margot. Her own eyes, small and brown, mocked them all.

"They're at a difficult age,'" Levanah excused. "Run along, children."

Released, they flashed her grateful looks and went out as sedately as they had come in.

"They're apt to be shy," Levanah said. "Do you find Sigrid difficult at school?"

"She's very good, very obedient," he said. It troubled him, that blank obedience, that prim little mouth and those downcast eyes. Sigrid had been a sweet-natured, gentle baby with much of Mary in her. Now her sweetness seemed to be iced by something he could not identify. Both his daughters looked at him as if he were a stranger whom secretly they despised. There was a heaviness at his heart when he rose to leave.

Levanah, having seen him out, sat down again in the drawing room, her chin on her hand, her yellow eyes thoughtful. She was astute enough to know when a man had no intention of falling in love with her, and she was not, she decided, sufficiently interested to waste her arts on changing his opinion. But her pride had been damaged. Franz von Braun would have to suffer for that.

She raised her head and whistled softly on a long-drawn-out breath. After a moment the two children ran in, their sedateness temporarily lost as they came.

"Has he gone? Did you want us?" Margot demanded.

"The car went so he must have gone," Sigrid commented. "Was it a secrets whistle, Aunt Levanah?"

"Yes, a secrets whistle," Levanah put out her hands and drew the little girl toward her. "But not a very happy secret, I'm afraid."

"Tell us," Sigrid said.

"Your father wants to take you away from Kingsmead," Levanah said.

"But he can't! Kingsmead is our home!" Sigrid exclaimed.

"Your father wants to find you a new mother," Levanah said.

"Our mother is dead and gone to heaven," Margot chanted.

"I meant—a stepmother," Levanah said. "He is going to Germany next summer to find you a stepmother."

"I don't want a stepmother," Margot said shrilly. "I don't want to leave Kingsmead."

"He won't listen to me," Levanah said sadly. "He won't listen to me or to Aunt Leah. He wants you to live at the Manor School."

"In the flat?" The elder girl's eyes were scornful. "It's a poky place!"

"Why can't you be our stepmother?" Margot inquired.

"Father could marry you and we could all live at Kingsmead," Sigrid said brightly.

"Your father doesn't like me," said Levanah.

The children stared at her. To them it was incomprehensible that anybody could dislike Levanah. Sigrid had retained only a faint recollection of Mary. For Margot Levanah was the only mother she had ever known.

"We won't go," Sigrid said. "We won't go with him."

"My dears, he is your father and has the right to take you."

"I will kick the stepmother," Margot said, narrowing her eyes.

"That will do no good," her sister said. "It will only make Father angry if he likes the stepmother."

"But she's not here yet," said Margot.

"She's not coming till next year," Sigrid said.

"Is he going to bring her back from Germany?"

"Next year will come sooner than you think," said Levanah.

"Then we'll have to do something," Sigrid said, glancing out of the corners of her eyes at Levanah's profile. "We'll have to do something, won't we?"

"In the cottage," said Margot hopefully. "Can we go to the cottage?"

"Not until dark of the moon," warned Levanah. "And Selena and Johnny mustn't know."

"Only us and Aunt Leah," Margot said happily.

"Will we make her ill?" Sigrid wanted to know.

"We don't know who she is," Levanah reminded them. "Your father will have to go to Germany to find her and bring her back."

"Then we must make *him* ill," Margot said, clapping her plump hands.

"We will talk about it later, at dark of the moon," Levanah promised.

The children looked at each other, smiling. This was the side of Levanah that fascinated them most, the secret part of her that woke them from their beds in darkness and took them across the fields to the white stone cottage buried deep in the woods near the river. Often Aunt Leah went with them, her face gaunt under the piled white hair, but it was Levanah who showed them what to do, and chanted deep in her throat in a way that made shivers go up and down Margot's spine. It was the secret that the four of them shared, the secret that made wishes come true and hurt the people one didn't like.

Franz, driving slowly down to the Manor School, stopped as Michael Shaw hailed him from the other side of the road. A warm friendship had grown up between the older and younger man, and the forty-five years between them was bridged by mutual respect.

"I've been for a stroll in the village, but I'd appreciate a lift back to the farm," Michael said, easing himself into the passenger's seat.

"You should take it easy," Franz admonished.

"A little gentle exercise never hurt. Giles has taken Wenna over to Maidstone. She wants to look at hats and he wants to look at a tractor, so they'll both be happy when they get back. Will you come in for a spot of whisky? A walk followed by a drop of hard stuff and a cigarette is guaranteed to cure the blues."

"Do you think I'm suffering from them?" Franz swung the vehicle over the low bridge.

"I think you're troubled about something," Michael said, easing himself to the ground as they stopped at the farm gate. "Come in anyway, and talk or don't talk, as you feel inclined."

Whittle Farm looked snugly prosperous, its windows gleaming, a fire laid ready for the evening. There was an air of unconventionality in some of the ornaments that pleased the eye. A long-legged black doll clad in a sarong rode on the back of a model swan. Several of Michael's canvases adorned the walls; flowers were hung in a straw basket; a vivid quilt was flung across the back of the sofa.

At his ease in the high-backed, deep-cushioned chair, Franz sipped at the generous measure of whisky, and smiled across at Michael.

"It's peaceful here," he said.

"Without being lonely, eh? You should think of taking another wife," Michael said. "Oh, I can see what's in your mind! 'What does the old fool know about it'? Fool is right! I spent too long after Beth Falcon died in mourning her memory. I was fortunate because when I came back to Maria Regina I found Wenna. If I were you I'd not wait for Fate to drop a ripe plum in my lap. I'd go seeking."

"For a wife? I'd not find another Mary."

"Give those two girls of yours a lively, sensible mother," Michael advised.

"You think they need one?"

"Wenna is—anxious about them," Michael said. "She's a practical woman, but she's also a Celt and like all Celts she has the occasional flash of intuition, second sight, whatever you like to call it. And she has been anxious about Sigrid and Margot for a long time."

"I too am anxious," said Franz, taking another mouthful of whisky.

"In what way?"

"The girls are too polite, too cool, too well behaved," Franz said slowly. "They greet me with a smile, Sigrid is very attentive in class, and all the time there is something I can't explain or understand. I can only describe it as a kind of—knowing."

"They are very fond of Leah and Levanah."

"Rightly so, if circumstances were normal, for Leah and Levanah have given them a home ever since Mary died."

"But you feel the circumstances are not normal?"

"Feel it without knowing why," Franz said restlessly. "It is partly the house, I suppose. So much has happened there over the centuries that it must have left its imprint, but it's more than that. There is something about Leah and Levanah that chills me too. I am certain they hate each other but there is no way of proving it, for they seem so close, so united in their opinions."

"Why not take Sigrid and Margot back to live

with you at the flat?" Michael suggested. "Margot is old enough to start school now, so what could be more natural than that you should wish her and Sigrid to make their home with you?"

"Levanah would oppose it."

"Levanah can do nothing to prevent it. You are the children's father and have the right to choose where they live. Once away from her influence and from the house, they will develop closer ties with you."

"Children are a problem," said Franz gloomily.

"I suppose they can be, though I have never thought of Levanah as my child," Michael said. "I feel no guilt about it for I never even knew of her existence until she was nearly grown up. I feel that Giles is more my child than she ever was."

"You did adopt him."

"Yes, indeed. He is now Giles Shaw of Whittle Farm. The farm will be his when Wenna goes, and the profits from my paintings are in trust for him. The little property in Wales will come to him too one day. You know tradition has it that the first witch to marry into the Falcon family came from that very same farm, and the witch blood has continued ever since. It's a fascinating story and there are still people who believe it. I have often thought of visiting the farm. Saron it is called. Wenna has not been back to her native land for many years, and it would give me pleasure to take her."

"Would Giles go with you for a visit?"

"That boy's heart is fixed in Kent," Michael said, "for Kent contains Whittle Farm and Selena Falcon."

"Levanah disapproves of that too."

"Levanah has *her* heart set on a lord for Selena,"

Michael said wryly. "A mere gentlemen farmer is no catch at all. I am sorry for it. When Selena is of age she will be able to marry where she chooses, but it would be a great pity to cause a rift in the family. There have been too many quarrels."

"But you and Wenna approve?"

"I believe the young must live life as they find it and make their own mistakes and successes," Michael said. "Wenna is fond of Selena. Oh, she is a little wild, but that is normal. It is a very great pity that Levanah did not allow her to train for a profession. Selena has energy and intelligence. It is being frittered away on parties and dances and visits to giggling girl friends, all designed to show Levanah that she won't knuckle under to maternal discipline. She would make a good wife for Giles, and a good mother."

His glance was a trifle wistful, as if he were remembering that both Selena and Johnny were his grandchildren. He had had no part in their upbringing either, but the shadow cast by the great house rested on them only lightly. There must be, Franz decided, more in them of their lighthearted, happy-go-lucky father than of their mother.

"I'll insist on Sigrid and Margot coming back to the flat," he said briskly.

"And find a good-tempered woman to marry. Bless me," said Michael, "but you're not yet fifty. At seventy-six I was enjoying a honeymoon."

"We haven't all got your stamina," Franz said, draining the last of his drink and rising. The company of his old friend had both refreshed him and strengthened his resolve. He would remove his children from Kingsmead and bring them back under his wing. And when summer came he would take a trip back to the little town where he had been born, and see if Kirsten was still there, and still unwed.

Levanah, going into the solar, found Leah in her usual seat by the window. The oak-paneled apartment had always been the older woman's favorite place. As a plain, gawky child she had crept here often to brood over fancied wrongs. As a young woman she had wept and schemed here. Now, in her seventieth year, she sat, with folded hands, looking out into the courtyard. Dusk had blurred her sharp profile and in the gloom her black dress was no more substantial than a shadow.

"Franz is thinking of taking another wife," Levanah said without preamble.

"So Sigrid told me." Leah turned her head toward her niece and laughed. "And it isn't you," she said, grimly triumphant. "He is not interested in you. He doesn't even like you very much."

"I could make him want me," Levanah said, "if I cared to take the trouble, but he's not worth it."

"You only wanted him because he was married to Mary," Leah said. "You only married Teddy because I hoped he'd marry Mary. And you only take care of Sigrid and Margot because they are her daughters!"

"Franz intends to go to Germany to look up a childhood sweetheart," Levanah said, continuing her own train of thought. "We will have to prevent his going."

"You don't mean that you intend to have him yourself, after all?"

"I told you I'm not really interested," Levanah said. "I don't want him."

"But he has to be punished for not wanting you," Leah said slowly. "That's what you mean, isn't it?"

"My own mother killed herself with no thought for me," Levanah said with sudden passion. "My own father never even knew that I'd been conceived. I grew up not being wanted."

"That isn't true. I cared for you, reared you."

"To walk behind your own daughter and Cousin Teddy, to be grateful for a roof over my head. And when I began to learn the extent of my own power, when I began to know the full meaning of the crescent moon on my thigh, then you sent me away as if I were unclean. You might as well have tied a bell around my neck!"

"You came back," Leah said faintly.

"Yes, I came back." Levanah spoke softly, triumphantly. "I came back and married Teddy. What agony it must have been, Aunt dear, to watch me walking up the aisle toward your nephew, while your precious daughter went flaunting around Europe with that unnatural friend of hers."

"You should have died instead of Beth," Leah said dully. "My sister was sweet and gentle and—"

"Killed herself after you told her that her lover was dead," said Levanah. "That was a very foolish thing to do. But you've done many foolish things, haven't you? We've done many things together."

"God knows I've been punished for it," Leah moaned. "I've been punished over and over."

"You're talking nonsense," Levanah said calmly. "Why, we are growing more prosperous with every spring, and you and I are such devoted companions that the whole neighborhood marvels at us. And you are going to help me keep Franz here in Marie Regina, unwed. You are going to help me, aren't you, Aunt Leah?"

"You know I always do," Leah said with the weariness of long hatred in her face and voice. "But they're *his* children. Is there any need to bring them into it too?"

"They need the training," Levanah said briefly.

"And if they tell?"

"They won't. That much they know already. Can I get you something? A nice cup of tea? You must be tired after such a long day, and you're not as young as you were."

"I'll outlive you!" Leah said suddenly and viciously. "That much I swear."

"You may at that," her niece said lightly, "but not for long, and you'd not enjoy it much."

Her leaving the room should have been a relief, but her musky perfume lingered on the air. Leah opened the casement and breathed in great gulps of night-scented breeze, but the aroma of musk was too strong, and her refuge had been invaded.

She closed the window and went slowly, pulling her black shawl about her, into the great hall and up the stone staircase. From the wall of the gallery the portraits of her ancestors gazed out indifferently. As a child she had liked to hear stories about them, but as the eldest of five children and the plainest of three sisters she had been expected to make herself useful and not waste time on fantasies.

At the end of the gallery, opposite her own room which adjoined Levanah's apartment, was the seldom-used sitting room where Beth had died. Staring at the closed door, remembering how the blood from her sister's wrists had soaked into the carpet, Leah began to shake in an intensity of fear and hate. From the hall below long shadows reached from the tapestries, mocking her bleak despair.

Chapter 11

The girls had been back at the flat over the Manor School for two years and, to all intents and purposes, had forgotten they had ever had any other home. They still went over to Kingsmead sometimes to spend a night there, however.

"They are such good company for Aunt Leah and me," Levanah said, "especially now that Selena has taken a flat in town."

Selena's engagement the previous summer to Giles Shaw had been greeted by those at Kingsmead with icy disapproval. Levanah had at first refused to acknowledge it at all. Now she referred to it as "that unfortunate affair" when she was obliged to mention it. Michael and Wenna had been warmly pleased. With Giles working full time on the farm and the wedding due at Easter they looked forward to a quiet old age.

"Wenna has had her hands full running the house," Michael confided. "She'll be glad to have a younger girl take over. We might take a trip, she and I, perhaps to New York. One of the galleries there is putting on an exhibition of my work."

Michael still did a little sketching from time to time and he was a familiar figure in the neighborhood, taking his daily stroll down to the village to buy his cigarettes or, on windless days, making his way slowly up the hill to where the ruins of the ancient monastery poked jagged stone into the sky.

Franz sighed, half in envy, as he lowered himself into an armchair. It seemed manifestly unfair that Michael should be so active for his age when he himself, at barely forty-seven, sometimes found the most exquisite agony in moving at all.

"Generalized rheumatism," the doctor had said briskly, and given him ointment to rub on his screaming joints.

There were days and weeks when he could move easily without pain, and there were other times when he could scarcely put his feet to the ground or hold a pen. It had been so bad on the one occasion he had set out to take his daughters to London for the weekend that he had been forced to turn back.

Occasionally he still toyed with the notion of going back to Germany to seek out his childhood sweetheart, but he had settled into a rut and the prospect of jolting across Europe like a middle-aged knight was losing its appeal.

The flat was comfortable and Sigrid, at eleven, was already a competent housewife with a liking for cookery. The duties of schoolmaster occupied most of his days and in the evening he frequently walked down to Whittle Farm for a drink and a chat with the Shaws. The atmosphere of their home was always warmly hospitable, and Michael's mind was still acute, though, in conversation, he had developed a habit of rambling around a subject.

Franz tried not to intrude too often on the privacy of their neighbors, and there were many evenings when he sat alone, correcting exercise books with one part of his mind while the other part was aware of the silence and loneliness about him. The children were asleep in the bedroom they shared just across the narrow landing.

He rose on an impulse and crossed into their room. Other children, he had been led to believe, demanded drinks of water and bedtime stories and had to be reminded to brush their teeth. His own daughters made their toilet methodically, bade him a sedate good night and went to sleep without any fuss. They were asleep now, lying still and straight under the unrumpled covers, their clothes neatly folded on the table between the twin beds. He looked down at the two sleeping faces, outlined in the light from the landing, wishing one of the girls would stir and wake and ask him for something, but they slept on, peaceful and self-sufficient.

Resigned, he turned away and, to create for himself the illusion that he was useful to his daughters, began to move noiselessly about the room, picking up objects and putting them down again in the same place. The room was neat and orderly as usual, and cold. He shivered slightly and thought that, with the summer almost at an end, he would cheat the cold winter ahead by taking the children away for Christmas. And as soon as spring came and the wedding of Selena and Giles was over, he would take that trip to Germany.

Pain stabbed him so viciously that he drew in his breath and caught at a small chest of drawers. The top drawer had not been closed properly and his fingers, clutching at its edge, pulled it out farther and tipped its contents onto the floor. Margot whimpered, her eyelids flickering, and then slept again, one plump arm flung above her head.

Franze stared down at the pile of sweaters and blouses with which the drawer had been filled. The garments had been carefully rolled up, but now one or two had unrolled in their descent, and a small doll had tumbled out.

A doll? Wincing with pain, he bent and picked up the object. It was made of wood, its face crudely painted, bits of lank gray wool glued to the top of its head. It reminded him of somebody, but for a moment he could only stare at it in bewilderment, at the sharp pins driven through the arms and legs. One of the wooden legs was shorter than the other. He looked from it to his own thick-soled boot and a fresh fit of shaking overcame him, as piece by piece the jigsaw fitted into place.

The girls still slept. He gazed at them, marveling at the innocent faces, the length of their lashes, their white-frilled nightdresses. He and Mary had conceived them in love. And they had become—his mind shivered from the word and an image of Levanah formed behind his eyes. The small, thin figure in the clinging black dress, the curving red hair, the narrow amber eyes, the delicate fingers on one of which the black pearl glowed. Each part of her shimmered in his imagination like the gleaming coils of some deadly snake.

He limped from the bedroom and went down the stairs as quickly as the pain would allow. Anger was mounting in him as strongly as the sexual excitement he had forced himself to subdue since his wife's death. He had not garaged the car and it started easily, the engine purring into life as if it too wished to aid him. On the seat beside him the wooden doll lay still and obscene.

Kingsmead glowed softly with the recently installed electric lights on which Johnny had insisted. Levanah had reluctantly agreed on condition that the great hall was untouched. Here oil lamps shadowed the corners and beamed light onto the heavy, dark furniture and stone-flagged floor. As was usual in summer the front door stood ajar, and he walked straight in without ringing the bell.

Levanah stood by the tall dresser, a silver-gilt cup in her hands. She glanced up as Franz came in and said coolly, "Good evening. I was just looking at this christening cup. It was given to one of my ancestors by Good Queen Bess. Astonishing to see how the centuries dwindle down. What brings you here? The girls are quite well, I hope?"

"*This* brought me!" He flung the doll on the dresser with a sharp cracking of wood. It lay, its eyes staring up, the long pins protruding grotesquely.

"What a horrid thing," Levanah said, putting back the cup and staring at the doll. Her eyebrows were raised and there was an expression of amused distaste on her face. "What is it?"

"You know what it is, and you know who it's supposed to be," Franz said grimly.

"How should I know? I am past the age for playing with dolls," she said lightly.

"That is no doll! Look at it! The gray hair, one leg shorter than the other."

"I must admit it does have a faint resemblance to you," she said slowly. "But who would do such a thing?"

"I found it in a drawer of the children's, hidden among their clothes."

"How exceedingly naughty of them," Levanah said.

"This is more than mere naughtiness," Franz said angrily. "These pins rammed into it—and my own joints so inflamed that there are days when I can scarcely move!"

"My dear Franz, this is 1932!" Levanah exclaimed. "You talk as if we all lived in the Middle Ages, and ran around casting spells by dark of the moon."

"Is that when you work?" he snapped.

"Dark of the moon, light of the moon—who cares or knows the difference? You are being ridiculous," she said.

"Am I? Then explain this to me."

"A childish prank that you are magnifying out of all proportion," she shrugged.

"This is no childish prank," he said. "This is sheer, calculated evil."

"It begins to look like it!" she said thoughtfully. "Mary was—"

"What has Mary to do with this?"

"I was only going to say that Mary was always a trifle—odd," Levanah said gently. "She did have a most peculiar relationship with that Charlotte Bishop. Is it possible that the oddity has come out in a different way in the children?"

"Mary is dead. Don't dirty her name," he said stonily.

"I was very fond of my cousin," Levanah said. "Nobody could have been more delighted when she came back here with you, married and with a baby. Reconciliation is a beautiful thing."

"Leave Mary out of it," he said again.

"Yes, of course. We were speaking of the children.

They must have made this in a fit of childish pique."

"Somebody carved this and told them what to do," Franz said.

"But who *could* it have been?" she asked, her eyes glinting laughter. "Who would know how to make such a thing?"

"Stop pretending!" he cried in sudden violent fury. "We both know who made this. I have lived here long enough to hear all the tales about the witch mark passed down through generations of Falcon women. You bear it yourself."

"I knew Germans were sentimental. I didn't know they were superstitious too," she mocked.

"*You* made that obscenity and told the girls to hide it," he accused. "Two years ago, when I took them back to live with me, you let them come too readily."

"As their father you have the right to take Sigrid and Margot where you please."

"You needed them close to me. Doesn't the victim need to be as near as possible?"

"How should I know? I never studied the subject," she said indifferently.

"You were probably born knowing it," he said bitterly. "Isn't it true that Leah sent you away when you were a girl? Mary told me something of those old rituals down in the old cottage. And then you came back. But why do you corrupt my children? Why not Selena and Johnny? Why mine?"

"All this talk of corruption," she yawned. "It is complete nonsense."

"It was because Mary was loved, wasn't it?" he said slowly. "Even poor Charlie Bishop loved her enough to die for her, and I loved her enough to marry her."

"Teddy married me."

"But you didn't love him. Unloving and unloved! That's it, isn't it? And then Mary died, and her children were yours to rear, and you corrupted them. Would it have gone on if I'd agreed to marry you? Would you have been content, knowing that you had everything that Mary loved? Would you have tried to corrupt me too?"

"Do keep your voice down," she said. "The servants may hear and they will probably imagine you've been drinking. You haven't, have you?"

"You can't even find the honesty to admit it, here when we're alone together."

"Admit what? You find a doll stuck with pins hidden away in a child's drawer, and you immediately jump to the conclusion that I am responsible for all your aches and pains! Is it likely that anyone would pay the slightest heed to such a farrago of nonsense?"

"I am taking Sigrid and Margot away," he said.

"You have every right. A little holiday would do you good," she said kindly. "Aunt Leah and I have not liked to mention it, but you have been looking very tired and strained recently."

"I am leaving Marie Regina for good," he interrupted. "I'm taking the children abroad. They are still very young and the harm that's been done can be undone."

"It is usual to give a term's notice," she said coldly.

"The circumstances are unusual. I shall be leaving first thing in the morning."

"You're being very foolish," she said softly, "and jumping to conclusions like a hysterical schoolgirl. Do look at me, Franz. Do I look like a woman who goes about muttering weird incantations and sticking pins into wooden dolls?"

She looked, he thought, fey and delicate, her skin milk-white under the smooth hair, her lips parted, her small breasts taut under the handkerchief-skirted black dress. The dark pearl on her left forefinger sent a shaft of reddish light toward him, and her eyes were gold-fringed.

"Wouldn't it be more fun to make love to me than some fat German cow?" she breathed.

"You're a bitch," he said, his breath harsh in his own ears. "God help any man who loved you. Teddy Falcon never knew how lucky he was when he was killed on the Somme."

The narrowed eyes glittered and she made a curious motion with her left hand as if she drew patterns on the air, but her voice was calmly pleasant.

"Then I see no point at all in furthering this discussion. You will not, I hope, expect a term's salary, as you're leaving without notice. I will have to advertise for a teacher, I suppose. You have made things very difficult for me."

"I'll leave the keys at Whittle Farm," he said abruptly and turned on his heel. As he went out the temptation to look back was a net spread to snare him. He paused for only an instant, his head bent, and then closed the door very quietly behind him.

Levanah remained where she was, her expression thoughtful. Even when she was unobserved she did not allow anger to distort her features, but her hands trembled slightly as she picked up the doll.

Sigrid and Margot had been stupidly careless to leave it where it could be found. She could not, however, entirely absolve herself from blame, for she had forgotten how young they were. She had also underestimated Franz von Braun. His gentleness, his lameness, his dislike of scenes and arguments had led her to discount both his intuition and his strength of will. Now, having guessed the truth, he would certainly leave Marie Regina and take the little girls with him. She would lose two most promising pupils and be deprived of the satisfaction of seeing Mary's precious daughters grow twisted like trees forced out of shape.

The doll stared up at her. She moved with it to the fireplace at the left of the staircase. The deeply curved hearth was laid with apple logs ready for lighting against the chill of the night.

Levanah knelt down and laid down the doll in the fireplace. Its head, adorned with the tufts of gray wool, stuck out at an angle. She reached for the matches, struck one and applied it to the logs and the screws of newspaper beneath. Then she sat back on her heels and whistled on a soft, clear note.

"Aunt Levanah wants us." Sigrid sat, waking instantly and sitting bolt upright in bed. From the other bed Margot said, her voice still blurred in slumber, "Who? What is it?"

"Margot, wake up! Aunt Levanah wants us to link in."

They habitually accorded Levanah the courtesy title of "aunt."

"I'm tired," Margot complained, knuckling her eyelids.

"Margot, get *up*!" Sigrid, out of her own bed, stared at the garments and the hanging drawer.

"What happened? Why do we have to link in?" Margot demanded crossely.

"I don't know, but we have to do it. Come to the window."

Margot reluctantly forsook the cocoon of warmth in which she had been luxuriating and joined her sister.

"Did someone find the mannikin?" she piped.

"I don't know. We can think about that later. Right now we have to link in."

Sigrid gave Margot a little push towards the window.

Levanah, warming her thin hands at the creeping blaze, felt Leah join her. The older woman crouched beside her.

"He found the doll," said Levanah. "He is leaving Marie Regina and taking the children with him."

"He can't do that. They are my grandchildren," Leah said in alarm.

"He will do it if he is not stopped," Levanah said.

"We must stop him," Leah said. "I lost Teddy and Mary. I can't lose Sigrid and Margot too."

"Be still and calm then," her niece commanded. "We cannot draw down the power unless we are calm."

"I can't lose the children too," Leah moaned.

"Be still," Levanah said.

Her eyes, glowing as yellow as the flames, fixed upon the doll. The pupils narrowed to slits and a tongue of fire licked along the painted wood.

Franz, reaction setting in after the unpleasant encounter, felt the intolerable aching in his joints spread through every bone. His nerves screamed with pain and his eyes ached as he peered through the windshield at the dark road ahead.

Behind him lay the bulk of stone that had been Mary's home. She had escaped from it once and he had brought her back to it, hoping to exorcise the ghosts of the past. It had been useless, and now Mary was dead and her children trapped in the web at Kingsmead.

"I'll drive them up to London first thing in the morning," he said aloud and defiantly. "We'll go to Germany. I can obtain a post there, teaching English. I'll send the girls to a good convent school. They are young still and will forget this foolishness. They are my children, mine and Mary's, and I'll not fail them." In his head laughter began, soft and sweet at first, and then growing louder and harsher, beating against the bones of his skull. His brain was bursting, splintering into fragments. He moaned, clapping his hands to his ears, his pain-wracked foot scrabbling vainly for the brake. The bridge loomed up, its parapet gleaming gray-white under the dark sky.

The car hit the low coping, seemed to hesitate for a moment as if it had a life of its own, and then plunged on, somersaulting as it went, smashing against one of the supports that reared up out of the shallow, summer-dwindled river, and burst into flames that not even the sweet-flowing water could instantly quench.

"It is finished," Levanah said and smiled with pure pleasure.

The wood of the doll was now indistinguishable from the wood of the apple logs. The fire blazed fiercely, shooting thousands of glowing sparks up the wide chimney breast.

"Are you certain?" Leah whispered. Sweat dripped down her white face onto her hands.

"I'm certain." Levanah rose and stretched, her mouth curving into a smile of pure contentment.

"I wish it had not been necessary," Leah said.

"Conscience sits uneasily on your tongue," Levanah said. "Shall we have a cup of tea? A nice cup of tea always makes you feel better."

"Someone ought to go down to the school," Leah said. "Those children are alone there."

"But we don't yet know that, do we?" Levanah's nails dug into her aunt's wrist. "As far as you and I are concerned, Franz drove over to ask me if I'd thought any more about hiring an assistant teacher to help him at the school. He left without taking any refreshment because he didn't want to leave the children alone too long."

"Will it be all right?" Leah, still crouching, looked up at her niece.

"Isn't it always?" Levanah said. "Now do let's have that cup of tea!"

"I'm thirsty," Margot said as they turned from the window.

"You're always thirsty," Sigrid said. "And if you're not thirsty you're hungry, and if you're not hungry you're wanting something else."

"I want lemonade and a bun," said Margot, flopping back into bed.

"I have to tidy up first," Sigrid said primly, beginning to roll up the spilled jumpers.

"Shall I call Father for a drink?" Margot asked.

"Don't be silly. He's not here," the older girl said.

"Is he dead?" Margot inquired with interest.

"Probably. Do you mind?"

Margot sat up, hugging her knees, and considered the question.

"We can go back and live at Kingsmead," she said. "It's better than here."

"He must have misjudged the width," Giles was saying. He had run up from the village, where he and several of the local farmers had been enjoying a drink at the end of the day's work.

"I saw it happen," someone called from amid the crowd. "He took his hands from the wheel. I saw him in the headlights. He went straight into the side of the bridge."

"Poor Mr. von Braun!" Rebecca Stone, who adored other people's tragedies, put her hands to her mouth and swayed a little.

"Somebody ought to fetch an ambulance."

"I'll phone from the farm, but it's the police who'll be needed." Giles, his face white under his tan, turned away. He felt slightly sick. Franz von Braun was more his parents' friend than his own, but he had always liked the quietly spoken teacher.

"I wonder if anyone is with the children," somebody said.

"They may have heard the crash, or seen the flames. The poor little things will be terrified!"

"I'll get the buggy and go up to Kingsmead."

"Lady Levanah will have to be told. She'll want to take the girls back with her, I suppose."

"Poor little orphans," Rebecca Stone said. "Poor little souls! What a mercy they have Lady Levanah."

"And Mrs. Leah," another voice reminded them.

"At least they won't be alone in the world," someone else agreed.

In the river below the flames were dying and a waning moon silvered the ripples.

Chapter 12

"It's time for me to leave," said Cat.

She spoke in her usual gentle manner, her hands occupied with the knitting of a long scarf that would repel the cold wind.

"Are you certain?" Her companion looked across at her.

"These two years," said Cat, "I've been certain it was time for me to leave. I said nothing because part of me wished to remain here with you, and part of me was afraid. But part of me has always known that I would go away one day."

"I have known it too," said Leone. Her blue eyes resting on the young woman were affectionate.

"I am twenty-six years old," Cat said simply. "It would be very pleasant to stay here with you for the rest of our lives, but there is some task for me to do elsewhere."

"In Marie Regina?"

"I think so," Cat said.

"You're sure it isn't that you want to make a dramatic appearance before your mother?"

"It was like that once," Cat said. "I used to wonder over and over why she had left me, why nobody at Kingsmead had ever been allowed to hear of my existence. I guessed I was born out of wedlock, but other children are born to unmarried girls and accepted into their families. And the Falcons were rich enough to ignore convention. I used to dream sometimes of confronting her, of asking her why she did what she did, of making her acknowledge me. I wanted to—belong."

"Your roots are here," Leone said.

"Are they?" Cat's tone was wistful. "I was born here and Aunt Catrin always told me that many of my ancestors left this place and went into England to marry their Falcon cousins. I was bred here in the hills, and some part of me will always be rooted here. But I've another life tugging at my heart, like a dream I dreamed long ago and almost forgot. Until I find out more about that other life I can never really truly belong here."

"There is more to it than that," Leone said shrewdly. Cat nodded, her green eyes thoughtful, a troubled pucker between her brows.

"There is some pattern to it all," she said slowly. "Everything that ever happened to me, from Aunt Catrin deciding to keep me to your coming, has been for a purpose. For years I've been aware there was something for me to do, something to set right. I don't know yet exactly what it is, but the time has come for me to find out. And I'll not do that by sitting at Saron year in, year out."

"So you'll rush down to Kent like a crusading angel, will you?" Leone asked with a touch of amusement.

"I'll go to London first," Cat said slowly. "The money that Aunt Catrin left for me will keep me for a little while, won't it?"

"For a couple of years, but why London?"

"Because I've never been farther than Chester in my life," Cat said. "I have a Welsh accent and country clothes and no idea how to dance or flirt. When I go to Kingsmead I want to be able to hold my own with my rich relatives."

"That's practical," Leone approved.

"Six months in London would teach me a little about fashionable society," Cat said eagerly.

"Are you going into England to perform some task or to find a Falcon cousin to wed?" Leone inquired dryly.

"Oh, I shall never marry." Cat's voice held confidence. "I'm really not much interested in men."

"There have been several sniffing around you in the past few years," the older woman reminded her.

"Sniffing around the farm more like," Cat scoffed. "It's a nice little property, and most folk don't realize that I'm not actually the owner. Anyway, men don't interest me at all. I made up my mind ages ago that I'm a born old maid."

Leone made no comment but her eyes studied the younger woman. Cat looked younger than her actual age, with something of the untouched innocence of a child in her candid eyes, but she was a woman for all that, breasts high and hips rounded, lower lips full and passionate. Her ink-black hair was coiled, like Leone's, at the back of her small head, and she moved gracefully, setting her narrow feet down like a dancer. It was inevitable that men would desire her, and only astonishing that so far she had remained heart free.

"If you're going to London and then on into Kent," she said at last, "you'll need to know a few things about your relatives."

"I know about the Falcons."

"Bits and pieces," Leone discounted. "I learned something of them from your Aunt Catrin, and I've made it my business to find out as much as possible since, mainly from old newspapers. I told you very little because I didn't want your seeing times to be colored by what I had related."

"But you'll tell me now," Cat said, laying aside her work and preparing to give full attention to her friend.

"I'll tell you now because the time has come, as you say, for you to leave. Facts only, and I beg you to curb that vivid imagination of yours and not interpret them too wildly."

"Facts then," Cat said.

"Very well. From your Aunt Catrin I learned that her sister's daughter, Margred, married her cousin, Harry Falcon. There were three girls and two boys born of that marriage. Leah, the eldest, married a man called Paul Simmons and was left a widow with a daughter, Mary. One of the sons emigrated; the other married and left a son, Teddy, whom Leah brought up. The two remaining girls never married but they both had children. Edith Falcon had a son whom she named Cal. Beth, the youngest, had a daughter, Levanah."

"Beth killed herself. I saw it long ago."

"When her baby was a few days old she cut her wrists and died," Leone said somberly. "So Levanah was reared with her cousins, Teddy and Mary, at

Kingsmead. Your aunt learned all this from her own daughter, Wenna, who taught in the school at Marie Regina."

"I know all this," Cat said impatiently.

"Listen to me," Leone urged. "When Levanah was a young girl she learned that her mother had bequeathed to her a small cottage on the estate. The cottage has always been know as Witch's Dower, and there are the usual tales around it of dark doings in the past. What seems certain is that Levanah used to go down to the cottage with Mary and Edith's son, Cal. Wenna wrote to your aunt about it. Apparently Levanah used to hold rituals in the place until Leah found out what was going on."

"And sent her away? I can remember Aunt Catrin mentioning that."

"Levanah went as a companion to a widow living in London," said Leone. "She was there for over a year. Shortly after she left the house was burned to the ground, and her employer was killed. She and a number of friends were down in the wine cellar when the fire began, and they were apparently cut off and trapped by the blaze. For a few days it was believed that Levanah had died too until she wrote to Leah saying she had decided to visit Saron for a while. Wenna wrote back to say how relieved they all were."

"And the fire? Was there something special about the fire?"

"According to the newspaper reports there was a feeble-minded girl employed as a housemaid. Unfortunately she died in the holocaust, and there was no clear way of determining the cause. The house was completely gutted, and the bottles of spirits in the cellar had exploded and made it impossible even to identify the victims properly. At all events Levanah was never questioned, or called upon to give evidence at the inquest."

"Go on." Cat's face was intent.

"Your aunt told me that Levanah stayed here until you were born. She made her swear never to tell the Falcons of your existence but to put you up for adoption as soon as possible. Then she returned to Kingsmead."

"And married her cousin, Teddy."

"Within the year," Leone said nodding. "Mary had quarreled with Leah and gone off on the Continent with a woman friend. Edith Falcon had died and her son had married Wenna."

"And then Levanah had twins."

"Selena and Johnny," Leone said. "Teddy and Cal died during the Great War and Levanah raised the children. Selena married Wenna's boy, Giles, a year ago. A big society wedding."

"I know, we read it in the newspapers. Didn't it say that Lady Levanah Falcon was ill and couldn't attend?"

"And no photographs were published, the family having 'a rooted dislike of publicity' " quoted Leone.

"Is there something more?" Cat asked.

"Only that Mary, Leah's daughter, married a schoolteacher several years ago and died in giving birth to her second child. Her husband was killed in a car crash about eighteen months ago, and the two children are now being reared at Kingsmead."

"But I saw it," Cat said slowly. "I saw the woman on a bed, having a child. There were two women with her and one of them had a ring set with a black stone on her left forefinger, Leone, I saw that!"

"You have a strong link with your family," the older woman said.

"The facts you've given me—" Cat hesitated and then plunged on. "I've heard most of them before, but strung out in order as you've just told them—Leone, is it just my vivid imagination or do you feel as I do that something is—wrong?"

"In what way wrong?"

"I don't know. I can't put my finger on it," said Cat. "I won't know until I meet the people, see the big house and the little white cottage. But I can smell evil, and I have a nose for evil."

"So have I," said Leone. "It is necessary for our own preservation that we should recognize the enemy."

"But who is my enemy?" Cat wanted to know.

Leone shrugged her broad shoulders.

"You will have to visit Marie Regina for that," she said. "There may be no enemy at all, but if there is you must recognize your foe and bind him—or her."

"I wish you would come with me," said Cat.

Leone shook her head. "I trained you," she said, "but you cannot go through the world holding my hand. This is something you must do alone, or not do at all, according to your judgment."

"I'll leave you in a week or two," Cat said, reaching for her knitting again.

Inside her a small coal of excitement had begun to glow.

It was blazing a fortnight later when she gazed from the windows of the flatlet she had taken across the tilted roofs of the capital.

Her original intention had been to stay at a hotel, but the thickly carpeted foyers and braided doormen had intimidated her. Instead she had rented a bed-sitting room with adjoining kitchen and bathroom at what seemed to her to be an exorbitant price. The apartment, however, was very comfortably furnished with a gas fire that gobbled up shillings, and London lay at her feet.

She stuck her head out of the window and coughed as specks of dust blew into her face. It was no wonder that city folk were so pale when they had to breathe this filth in and out all day! The food displayed for sale in the markets looked dusty too. She had never seen such miserable-looking apples or such wrinkled oranges.

But these were trifling matters set against the excitement of crowded streets and buildings that towered so high she had to tilt her head to see their tops. She had already discovered the river and spent an enthralling afternoon going up and down in a pleasure steamer crammed with tourists. She had explored the Tower with its grisly relics of a bygone age, and ventured into the Egyptian Gallery of the British Museum, where the bandaged mummies induced in her such an eye-pricking sadness that she had speedily come away again. She had taken an omnibus out to Kew Gardens, where the flowers had shapes she had never imagined and names she could not pronounce.

She was conscious, however, as the days went by, of a new and unpleasing emotion. She had never moved among so many people before, and paradoxically she had never been so lonely. Folk didn't seem to have any manners in the city, she decided crossly, after her bright "Good morning" to a passerby had met with a frosty stare for the third time. Everyone seemed to be in a hurry and to know exactly where they were hurrying. Nobody stood still to look at anything, though the sunset over the river was so pretty that she caught her breath in what was almost pain.

But the loneliness was hard to endure. She hoped it was not some lack in herself that stopped people from making friends with her. Odd, but on the farm with Leone, and the sheep bleating on the slopes of the hills, she had never felt the need for friends.

She wrote to Leone describing the sights, but not mentioning her loneliness. Her friend had probably guessed already and it did no good to moan. Meanwhile, having walked and ridden for hours every day, she returned to her apartment when dusk fell with aching feet and a headache that made it easier to be alone.

At the back of her mind the family she had never seen waited, like images on a screen, images with blank faces whose names she had only heard. Leah, Levanah, Wenna, Giles, Selena, Johnny. Wenna was married to an artist, a very old gentleman named Michael Shaw. That much she knew already, and she spent one day wandering about the art galleries in the hope of seeing some of his work, but the number of canvases muddled her and the acres of marble tiles made her legs ache.

She had been a month in London before she felt sufficiently confident to venture into a store and buy some clothes. Skirts were longer this season, the sales assistant told her kindly. Coats had big collars trimmed with fur and hats were cloches or slouched with tiny eye veils. Even respectable women were wearing low-cut satin evening gowns with narrow shoulder straps, and had their lips and nails painted a matching coral.

"I bought a green dress with a scalloped hem, and a coat in the same shade with a fox-fur tie," she wrote to Leone. "I bought an evening gown too, in dark red velvet. I'm afraid the color is a trifle vivid, but the girl in the shop said it suited my hair. I bought two afternoon dresses too. They have tea dances here in many of the restaurants. People can go in and eat their tea at a small table and listen to a string orchestra, and if they are asked, or have an escort, there is space in the middle of the floor for dancing. I am trying to pluck up the courage to go to one of these occasions, as they do seem to be very elegant."

The letter seemed, when she read it over, to be crammed with trivialities. She dashed off a postscript. "I think I am losing my country bumpkin air, and I will soon be ready to visit Kent. I am not sure when that will be. I only know that something will tell me when the time has come."

Meanwhile she tried on her new clothes, paid an unsatisfactory visit to a hairdressing salon, where she resisted all attempts to have her hair cut and marcelwaved, watched the sunsets over the river and kept herself from smiling at strangers.

It was April before she plucked up courage to enter one of the large restaurants where tea dances were being held. It was not, she told herself, that she intended to dance, but she looked forward to watching other people.

The table to which the waitress showed her was next to a pillar and her view was restricted, but the table with its white cloth and fringed red napkins was elegantly laid with china crockery. She ordered tea and cucumber sandwiches and slid her arms out of the new coat. She was wearing one of the two af-

ternoon gowns she had bought, the green of its pattern of tiny leaves exactly matching her eyes. Her
hair, despite the blandishments of the hair stylist,
was still coiled into a heavy knot, and at the last moment she had rubbed off most of the scarlet lipstick.

What she did not realize, as she sat sipping the
amber brew and tapping her foot idly in time to the
music, was that, in contrast to the women around,
there was a fresh eager quality about her. It revealed
itself in the curve of her mouth, in the slant of her
eyes, the way in which she held herself.

The young man who had just sauntered in, and
was engaged in casting a practiced eye over the
unattached women, was caught and held by the
glance of her bright eyes. For a moment he thought
the smiling gaze was for him, but the young woman
was watching the few couples revolving on the floor.

There was, he decided, good breeding in those
high cheekbones and that small head set on the slender neck. Her hair would be beautiful if it were released from its tight coils, and her eyes were as green
as a cat's, their corners uplifted.

Cat became aware gradually that she was being
studied with close attention. She turned her head and
met blue eyes in a handsome, high-colored face. For
an instant her heart gave a queer little leap as if she
were on her way downstairs and had missed a step.
Then, forgetting her newly acquired city manners,
she gave him her warm, welcoming smile.

"Good afternoon. May I join you?" His voice
was pleasant and there was a vacant chair at the other
side of the table.

"Yes, of course," she said, and he sat down, ges-
tured to the waitress and ordered tea with a casual

air that suggested he was used to entering restaurants and introducing himself to strange ladies.

"Perhaps I may be allowed to keep you company until your friend arrives," he said.

"I'm not waiting for anyone," she said innocently. "I only came in to have my tea and watch the people dance."

"Would you like to dance?" he asked.

"Oh no! I never learned," she said quickly.

"It's not difficult. Come on and I'll show you. I'm Eddie Weston, by the way."

"Catrin—Evans." She had better get accustomed to using the surname she and Leone had decided upon.

"Hold on to me," he ordered genially, "and do what I do in reverse."

It was easier than she had feared, though she stumbled occasionally and once trod quite hard on his foot. But he held her carefully, matching his stride to her own, talking to her every time she was tempted to look down on the floor, and her natural sense of rhythm took over so that after a little time, she began to enjoy herself, to listen to the music, to feel the warmth of him close to her.

"Did you say something to me?" she asked.

"I was asking if you were a visitor," he said.

"Oh yes. I'm staying in London for a few months," she said.

"Do you work here, in the city?"

"No, I don't work—at least, I'm—I'm studying," Cat said. She had been in London long enough to realize that most girls had a job of some kind.

"I'm going to fly," he told her.

"Oh, do you have to go?" Disappointed, she stared up at him, her arms dropping to her sides as the music ended on a flourish of violin strings.

"I meant I'm going to train as a pilot, an aircraft pilot," he said laughing. "But I'm here on a visit for a few weeks too. Are you enjoying yourself?"

"Yes." A day earlier that wouldn't have been true, but she was suddenly quite sure that nobody in London was having as good a time as she was.

A little breathlessly, as they sat down again, she said, "It's like ships, isn't it?"

"Ships?" he asked, puzzled.

"Yes, you know. Ships that pass in the night. You and I."

"Are we indeed? Shall I tootle my siren and pass on, or shall I have some more tea and you tell me all about yourself?"

"Let's not tell each other anything about ourselves," she said. "We're visitors, not likely to meet again."

"As milady pleases." He gave a mock bow. "But you're not going to drink your tea and vanish, are you? I'd rather like to take you out this evening. The new Garbo film is on. You like Garbo, don't you?"

"Oh yes, indeed I do." She and Leone never missed a Garbo film.

"Will you come with me then? I'm very respectable, with the most honorable intentions."

The blue eyes teased her. She had an impulse to reach out and touch his brown hair. Instead she folded her hands tightly in her lap, and said primly, "I'd like to see the Garbo film very much."

"It's settled then." He glanced at her as she drank her tea, wondering how old she was. In her twenties probably, but her manner was unsophisticated. He wondered if she were convent-bred. That would account for the endearing gaucheness. But even as he formulated this theory, her eyes met his over the rim of the teacup, and he was struck by an ageless wisdom in their depth.

I am going to fall in love with her, he thought, not with the feeling of anticipation that usually heralded one of his brief flirtations, but with a calm certainty as if everything had been settled between them.

Cat, watching him, felt a trembling warmth invade her thighs, and her nipples grow hard under the thin silk of the new dress. Emotions she had read about but never experienced flooded her being.

In an odd jerky voice she said, "They are playing another tune. What is it?"

"A tango. Would you like to try it?"

He looked at her doubtfully, but she cried, "Oh yes! I'm sure I can manage the steps." And felt herself in that moment to be capable of anything.

Chapter 13

They had been out for supper and, the evening being mild, were strolling along the Embankment. The river was gentle tonight and the rising moon arched her bow across a mist-softened sky. From downriver came the occasional mournful hoot of a foghorn or the falsetto chatter of a tugboat's whistle.

They walked in silence, their hands loosely linked, their footsteps in ringing harmony on the pavement. Earlier in the day there had been a demonstration of unemployed miners and bits of placard were scattered in the gutter. Cat, who had watched the silent procession of bitter-faced men, shivered, and Eddie put his arm about her.

"Cold?"

She shook her dark head, but leaned closer.

"I was pitying all the folk who haven't had a meal today," she said, "a *good* meal. Sometimes it hurts a little for me to have so much and others so little. I never realized, until I came to London, what a bad state the world was in."

181

"At least there'll never be another war." There was the faintest tinge of regret in his voice. "Germany learned her lesson."

"I hope you're right," she said, "but we're moving into the age of Aquarius, you know that. That means a period of great upheaval."

"I'm sure it does," he said indulgently.

She talked a lot about astrology and cosmic forces, and half the time he was not certain what she was on about, but he liked to hear her talk.

"It's true," she insisted. "Everything goes in cycles, like a pendulum swinging, and we have to try to right the balance."

"Which you do beautifully."

"Oh, do be serious!" Half-vexed, half-laughing, she broke away and put up her hands to fend off his kiss.

"I am serious. You speak a lot of good sense, and your principles are very high, and I want you to marry me."

He too had begun jokingly, but the last sentence came out in a rush.

"Marry me?" She stopped, her back against the railing. "But it's only a week—one week since we met. You don't know me."

"I know that you are good and gentle and beautiful," he said. "I know that I have met the one woman I want to spend the rest of my life with. I know it's very sudden, but something doesn't have to be slow in order to be true, does it?"

"No. No, it doesn't."

"It was a kind of recognition," he said.

"Yes. For me too." Her breath beat hard and short in her throat.

"Then we don't have to explain anything to each other. We know how we feel."

"Yes. Yes, we do."

"And you'll marry me? Say you'll marry me."

"I'll marry you," she said, and her lashes were wet.

"Dearest Cat!" His arms were around her and his mouth demanded a response. She gave it passionately, desire shuddering along her veins.

"I loved you when I first saw you, sitting in that damned restaurant, with your foot tapping and your eyes shining like twin candles."

"You don't know about me." She made a lazy, feeble protest. "I come from a tiny farm in the back of nowhere."

"You came from the sweetest corner of my favorite dream," he contradicted. "You will marry me?"

"Yes. Yes." She whispered the words as if they were so delicate that they might fall to earth and splinter.

"Soon. I want to marry you very soon. We can go to my home and be wed in the little church there. It's very old and beautiful."

"Whatever you please." She had never known such a sense of belonging.

"Lord, I forgot to tell you!" He drew away slightly, his face a comical mixture of pleasure and chagrin.

"That you have a wife and six children already?" she teased.

"Nothing so serious," he said.

"What then?" she asked.

"It's simply that—I'm not exactly what I said I was. What I mean is that I use the name Eddie Weston when I'm in town, but in actual fact I'm a—well, I'm a lord. Lord John Falcon. It's a sort of hereditary title passed down in our family ever since one of my ancestors kicked up her heels for Charles the Second. I don't mind it, but being a lord does cramp one's style. But we're all terribly ordinary at home."

"I'm sure you are."

Her whole life was crumbling about her, and she stood there saying calmly, "I'm sure you are."

"Wanting to be an aircraft pilot isn't considered the sort of career a peer of the realm ought to want to take up," he apologized. "My friends generally call me Eddie—my second name is Edward after my father!"

"Oh, indeed," she said politely.

"My family call me Johnny. You'll like my family. I've a twin sister, Selena, who's married to a sort of cousin of ours. They farm about three miles from us. My mother and my great-aunt still live in the big house, and a couple of my orphan cousins are being brought up there. But the estate is a decent size, so you'd not bump into one another."

His words made no sense. She heard each one clearly without being able to relate it to what had gone before. She was so cold that her skin prickled.

"We can travel to Marie Regina at the end of the week—that's the name of the village where we live. Very pretty but a bit dull. However, we don't have to spend all our time there. I have rooms in the city and we can travel. Would you like to visit Paris?"

"Yes, indeed."

"Paris is a superb place! Lots of—" He had been going to say "girls," but substituted, "chestnut trees and old buildings and lots of good food. I like

French food, though I never managed to learn how to speak the language."

"Oh." Her lips were stiff, shaping the monosyllable with difficulty.

"We'll buy the ring tomorrow. Do you fancy a solitaire or a cluster?"

"A solitaire," she said.

"What about your own people? Do you *have* people? You've never said."

"No. No—family."

"Lord, no mother-in-law to worry about! Oh, that didn't sound very nice, did it?" He looked at her contritely. "Truly? You've nobody at all?"

She shook her head.

"Well, you have now. You'll have me for the rest of your life."

She said nothing, but went on staring at him. The color had vanished from her face and her eyes were shadowed.

"I say, are you feeling all right?" he asked suddenly. He had never proposed to a girl before, but he had imagined a livelier response.

"I'm surprised," Cat said, and marveled at the lightness of her voice.

"I'm surprised at myself," he admitted, "but it's right to do it. It's right for me to love you. Why, it's almost as if someone or something up there had planned this, had arranged to bring us together out of all the millions of people in the world! Are you sure you're all right? You don't look well."

"The supper was a little rich," she evaded. "And this street lighting is unflattering anyway."

"We'll hail a taxi," he said. "You know, I'll have to think about getting a car to run about in here. I keep mine at home and rely on cabs, but it would be fun to have our own transport when we're in town."

The evening was blurring. As they got into the taxi she pressed her hand hard into the sharp edge of the ashtray on the door. The pain brought everything back into focus again. She was wearing the dark red dress and an evening coat of a pale ivory shade. She had eaten lobster and veal in a cheese sauce, and she and Eddie no, *Johnny*, had danced in between courses.

He had put his arm around her. She could feel its masculine hardness about her shoulders. His mouth was hard upon her mouth again, and his tongue was thrusting between her teeth. Her limbs were slackening and the world was floating away again.

"No! No, Johnny!" She wrenched herself away and shook her head violently from side to side.

"I only thought—as we're going to be married anyway."

"I think it would be better to wait," she said.

"Yes, of course." He drew her to him again, kissing her more gently. He respected her for her refusal, but his desire for her was unabated.

"I'll call for you at eleven o'clock tomorrow morning. We can choose the ring and celebrate with a champagne lunch."

"Yes. At eleven."

She spoke mechanically, dreading the moment when they would arrive, wishing that this nightmare journey were at an end.

The cab drew up at the steps of the tall building in which her flatlet was. She began to talk rapidly, her hands still in his.

"Don't bother to get out. You go on to your place. I'm going to flop straight into bed and sleep off my supper."

"Until eleven tomorrow—no, *today*. It's past midnight already."

"Until eleven," she echoed.

His kiss hurt her more than anything had ever hurt her in her life, and then, abruptly, she was quite calm and serene. She opened the door, stepped down to the pavement, slammed the door, blew a kiss. His head nodded toward her; his hand was raised in a cheerful salute. The cab drove away slowly, gathering speed as it reached the end of the street.

Cat stood, one hand at her throat where the high collar of the ivory coat was closed with a rhinestone buckle. Aloud she said, "Goodbye, Johnny," and was conscious of an overwhelming relief as the taxi turned the corner.

The steps were narrow and uneven, and the front door with its stained glass panel needed a coat of paint. She let herself into the hall and began to climb the two flights of stairs to her apartment. As she climbed she ticked off each stair in her mind as if it were overwhelmingly important.

Her room was chilly, and looking round as if she saw it for the first time she realized that, since her arrival, she had done nothing to make it more homely. Her new clothes and the few old ones she had brought filled the wardrobe and chest of drawers. She had hung no pictures and bought no books apart from a few shiny magazines that lay on the table. The room was a reflection of nothing. She took off her coat and eased her feet out of the Louis-heeled sandals in which she had practiced walking gracefully. On the farm she usually wore gum boots or sensible brogues. Then she sat in the armchair, her feet together, her back very straight, as if she were expecting company.

Little by little, like some malignant disease, the pain invaded her. She had not known such agony existed, and after a little while it became impossible to sit still. She began to walk up and down, up and down, while the walls pressed in on her.

A week ago she had been happy and not even known it. She had been smug in her own self-suffi-ciency. Now she could never go back and be as she had been before. Her life had been changed and her whole nature colored by an experience so shattering in its intensity that she wondered how she could ever have imagined she had been alive before. And it was all gone, destroyed in a few sentences. She might live as long as Aunt Catrin had done, in which case she would have to endure seventy more years of this silently screaming agony. Even worse was the thought that the pain would dull and the day come when she could no longer see Johnny's face clearly or hear his voice.

Her own grandmother had known this anguish of separation and escaped from it. There had been times when, looking at the face of the girl with the moon-stone ring, Cat had felt impatient hostility, but now she envied Beth Falcon her long sleep of death.

If she turned on the gas fire and didn't light it sleep would come for her too. She bent and twisted the jet, but no hissing sound escaped. Of course, she remembered now, the wretched meter had run out of coins while she was dressing to go out, and she had no change.

Aspirins! The newspapers were full of stories about girls taking overdoses. She had a small bottle somewhere, and scrabbled in her handbag. Purse, keys, a postcard to Leone she had intended to post, lipstick, compact. Sobs escaped her as she rummaged, though her eyes were dry.

If she stayed here a moment longer she would go insane. She flung her everyday coat over her evening dress and snatched up her handbag. She would go out again, back to the Embankment. To die in this cheerless room lacked dignity. The doors on the other landings were closed, the bulbs dim in their sockets. Except for the landlady who collected the rent every Friday she had never spoken to any of the neighbors. Perhaps, at this moment, they were all engaged in killing themselves or in thinking about it.

In the street she began to walk rapidly in the direction of the river. There were still plenty of people about, couples mainly with arms entwined, and here and there a group of young men on the lookout for female company. One man called an invitation out of the shadows, but she walked on unheeding, and he set an unsteady course for Leicester Square in the hope of more compliant game.

It was quiet down by the river, with the roar of the traffic muted. A little breeze rising from the surface of the water ruffled her hair, blowing small tendrils about her brow.

She walked down some steps and stood, her hands thrust deep in her pockets, staring at the water. It was deep and dark here and she had never learned how to swim. Staring at it she thought, *They will say I did it because I was of unsound mind. But that isn't true. People only destroy themselves in a flash of sanity, when they see everything clearly and so make a choice. Out of all the people in the world I met and fell in love with my own half brother, and I can't stop loving him or get away from the pain of it.*

She took a step nearer, her heels skidding on the damp stone. She could not even remember having put her shoes back on. If only there were some sense to the pattern she might, even now, draw back.

The moon reflected on the surface of the water was distorted, its curve jagged, its points blurred.

"If you're going to jump in," said a voice from the shadowed angle of the steps, "better to take your coat aff first. Pity to waste a nice bit of cloth."

The voice had the singsong accent of mid-Wales and was hoarsely masculine.

It had frightened Cat so much that she almost overbalanced into the reflected moon. As she teetered on her heels the man came to her side, grasping her arm and urging her to the drier stone.

"Haven't got a cigarette with you, have you, love?" he asked, sitting down again.

"Yes. Yes, I think so."

There was a crumpled pack in her pocket. She fished it out and gave it to him, and he drew out two cigarettes, lit them both and handed one to her.

"Ah, yes. Pity to spoil them with seawater, isn't it?" he remarked. "Better sit down for a few minutes while we have our smoke."

"You're Welsh," she said shiveringly, joining him as he made room on the step.

"From Llanelly," he nodded. "From your voice I'd say you were Welsh yourself. From the north?"

"Snowdonia."

"Very pretty they tell me it is there," he said approvingly. "But they're a funny lot, the North Walians, clannish."

"Were you with the big march today?" she asked.

"Came up from home to lobby members of Parliament," he said. "Bit of a farce with the mounted police charging into us and not a member of Parliament to be seen! Still, it was a nice change being in the fresh air, and some women came round with soup. I start off home in the morning. The wife gets fretful, see, if I leave her too long."

He coughed abruptly, the cough she had heard from the mouths of quarry workers at Dinorwic.

"Are you sick?" she asked.

"Got a touch of the old chest," he said. "Very bad it gets sometimes. The doctor told me last winter I'd got the worst lungs he'd ever seen for my age. 'Pitted with coal dust,' he said. Well, I could have told him that! Gave me some pink stuff to take and told me to go to a mountain resort for the winter. On eighteen shillings a week and five children under sixteen! Mad as a hatter—English, of course."

"I'm sorry," she said.

"Be a funny old world if everything was perfect," he said cheerfully. "Mind, there's been times when I've wanted to walk away, to get on the road between the houses and walk until I couldn't see the damned slag heaps anymore. Then my eldest runs up and tells me he's won a scholarship to the County School. No going down the pit for my Dewi! And I look up and the slag heaps have grass growing on them and little flowers like crowds of stars. Now, you—" He paused and then said, "Now, you must have some terrible trouble to be jumping into the cold river."

"I fell in love with a man and then discovered he was my own half brother," Cat said, and broke into a pattern of weeping.

"Annwyl mawr!" he exclaimed. "Now there's interesting."

"Interesting!" She raised her head, sobbing indignantly. "My life is ruined, finished."

"Ah yes, that's true enough," he agreed. "But it's still interesting! Now, if something like that happened to me, I'd be wanting to stay around and see how the ending came out."

"I told you. How can there be an ending except pain and more pain?"

"But the reason for it," he said slowly. "There is always the reason for the thing to happen, and often many years to pass before we can look back and see it plain. And when we look back we can often see why something had to happen before something else happened. Like digging away the rock and the rubble to get at the good, black coal underneath."

"The will of God," she mocked.

"I'd not be saying that," he said cautiously. "People are very fond of saying something is the will of God, when they mean they can't be bothered to do anything about it. Change what you can and try to find a reason for the rest of it."

"It hurts," she said. "It hurts too much to bear."

"Shows you're alive," he said and coughed again. "Shows you're a human being, still breathing, still asking questions. Only the dead have no curiosity."

"I never asked your name," she said, fumbling for a handkerchief.

"Dan," he told her. "Dan Gabriel. My grandfather was a Romany, see. They take fancy surnames."

"Gabriel," Cat said. "He was a messenger too."

"I'm no archangel," the man said. "I like my pint on Saturday, and a bit of singing at harvest festival."

"I have some money. It will pay for food on your way home."

He accepted the two pounds she thrust out with no

false pride, merely remarking, "And you'll be going home yourself now, I take it, or will you still be jumping in?"

"I'll be going home," she said, and stood up.

The pain was still almost unendurable, but there had to be some reason for it.

He made no further remark but she could feel his good will reaching after her as she climbed back up to the road. As she walked along she forced herself to plan calmly.

The landlady had not inquired Cat's home address, being apparently content if she received her money on time. And the rent had been paid in advance up to the following Friday. She would pack her things and catch the first train home in the morning. When Johnny came to collect her it would be as if she had never existed at all—but it was useless to think about Johnny.

Better to think about the farm where the slow summer was beginning, and of Leone's pleasure at seeing her again. She would say nothing to Leone about Johnny. She would simply say that the time was not yet ripe for her to go to Marie Regina. Perhaps now it would never be the right time, for she could not bear the thought of seeing Johnny again and of telling him the truth. Yet, if she were not meant to meet her family, why had she been plagued since childhood by fleeting visions of events at Kingsmead?

Against her will she began to wonder about the reasons for what had happened to her, but there were no answers, only the constant pain of loss that grew more piercing with every step she took.

It took only an hour to pack her belongings, and not even the false dawn had pearled the sky when, clad in her blouse and skirt and the new tweed coat, she sat down in the armchair. There were about three hours to go before she need set out for the station.

Such a short time had passed and she had lived an eternity of joy and horror. She felt immeasurably old, and so weary that it was an effort to raise her hand. Even the pain had dulled and lay upon her like a heavy weight.

Deliberately, as if she were performing some ritual, she closed her eyes and built up Johnny in her mind. He had been tall, with wide shoulders and long legs and well-shaped hands. His features had been strong, his eyes blue, his brown hair thick and wavy, springing from a broad forehead. His teeth had been blunt and white, his voice pleasant. He had smelled of soap and sharp cologne, and of something else she could not name but could only identify as maleness.

When he was complete in her mind she flooded herself with love for him. She beamed out love toward him until she was empty of everything. The emptiness lasted a few seconds only and then the pain crept back again and she crossed her arms tightly about herself rocking to and fro as if she were nursing a baby.

She woke without realizing for a few minutes that she had slept. The sun was shining and her first thought was the joyful, *This morning Johnny and I are going to choose my engagement ring.*

Then she remembered and the dull misery began to gnaw at her again. She rose, moving carefully as if she might break, and picked up the suitcases and went resolutely down the stairs.

Chapter 14

"I am beginning to believe that both my offspring are monsters!" Levanah said.

"Surely not, with such a charming mother," Leah said. "Dear aunt! How well you know me!" Levanah reached across and patted the older woman's arm. "But just think of Johnny and Selena for a moment. Didn't I give them both an excellent education, every possible advantage, all the things their father would have wished?"

"Yes. Yes, I have to grant you that," Leah admitted.

"So generous of you to say it!" Levanah's smile flashed out and was instantly gone as she reverted to her complaint. "And after all I've done Johnny doesn't take the smallest interest in the estate. I cannot understand it. He used to take a pride in his home, but for these past eighteen months he has spent more of his time above the ground than on it. If he had a wife and heir then he might be justified in risking his neck, but he shows not the faintest interest in getting married."

"He's young," Leah excused.

"He's twenty-five years old and the last male Falcon," Levanah said.

"You forget Giles."

"*Giles.*" Levanah's voice hardened. "Giles is not a Falcon at all, save by accident of birth. Do I have to remind you he is the son of your sister's bastard, and that he has even relinquished the name itself since my father adopted him? Selena's child will be a Shaw."

"But with Falcon blood."

"Oh, I grant you that," Levanah said. "And how much of the baby is either of us likely to see with Giles and Selena dragging it off to Australia?"

"My brother Price went to South Africa," Leah said. "We never heard of him again."

"Damn your brother Price! We are talking about Giles and Selena. The fool declares that a few years on the other side of the world will enable him to farm Kentish soil more effectively."

"Cannot Michael or Wenna persuade him?"

"Everything Giles does is quite perfect in their eyes," Levanah said bitterly. "Michael thinks more of Wenna's boy than he does of me, his own daughter! Not that one can entirely blame him for that since, thanks to you, he never even knew of my existence until I was grown up!"

"What about the farm?"

"They're putting a manager in to run it, and Wenna and Michael are going back to live there. Which means I have to advertise for another teacher in time for the autumn term. It's a blessing in a way, because Wenna really is too old now for the job, but she will insist she can run everything."

"You were very glad to have her take over after Franz had—died."

"As a temporary measure." Levanah drummed her thin fingers impatiently. "Her methods are old-fashioned, and she's past retirement anyway. She ought to devote what's left of her life to Michael."

"He seems to thrive," Leah said mildly.

"Yes, he's disgustingly long-lived." Levanah dismissed her father's state of health and returned to Giles and Selena like a terrier worrying a bone. "They both declare they will travel next summer. We will have to prevent them, that's all!"

"Oh no!" It was a cry of protest. "I'll not do any more. Not after Franz!"

"You have a tender conscience suddenly," Levanah said. "It got what you wanted, didn't it? Sigrid and Margot are very happy with us."

"Everything you want," Leah moaned. "You take everything you want."

"Not always," said Levanah. "When I was a child I wanted to know who my father was and how my mother had died, and you wouldn't tell me. I wanted Franz to marry me and he refused. No, I don't always get everything I want."

"But if Giles and Selena are determined to go, how can it be safely prevented?"

"I shall have to think about it," Levanah said tranquilly.

Leah rose and went restlessly to the window, where she stood looking out at the courtyard. Nothing about that courtyard had changed in four hundred years, though its cobbles were worn almost smooth, and water was now drawn up from the well only on the rarest occasions. But the ivied walls still rose on three sides and through the wide arch where the family carriage had once rolled she could see the drive curving between ancient oak and elm.

A figure was strolling up the drive. For a moment she thought it to be Giles, but this man was taller, and walked more briskly. Her spectacles, which she had only just begun to wear permanently, had slipped down the bridge of her nose. She pushed them into place and gripped the edge of the window frame as the figure came into focus.

"What did you say?" Levanah glanced up.

"Price! My brother Price—"

"The one who went off to South Africa? What of him?"

"He's here," Leah said in a breathless whisper, "walking into the courtyard."

"What on earth are you talking about?" Levanah rose from her chair and came to join her aunt. "Who is that man?"

"I tell you, it's my brother Price."

"Don't be ridiculous!" Levanah snapped crossly. "Your brother must be about seventy years old if he's still alive. That man can't be more than thirty."

"He's coming to the front door," Leah breathed.

"Then come away from the window and stop gaping," Levanah ordered. "No doubt he'll ring the bell and Molly will announce him."

As if on cue the bell jangled through the house. Leah started violently and fled to her seat.

"Lady Levanah, there's a gentleman here asking for Mrs. Leah."

Molly, who had just been promoted to the dizzy heights of parlormaid, twisted her hands nervously in the lace of her apron.

"Did he give a name?" asked Levanah.

"He says his name is Price Falcon, milady," Molly said.

Leah's face turned as white as her hair, Levanah smoothing her own red hair, said calmly, "Show him in, Molly, and then bring in some coffee—and do *try* not to rush everywhere."

"Yes, milady." Molly disentangled her fingers from the lace, bobbed out into the hall, and bobbed back a moment later, announcing, "Mr. Falcon to see you, if you please."

The stranger was tall and broad, with the creased blue eyes and sunlicked hair of an outdoor man. He approached with outstretched hand and an air of slightly brash confidence.

"Would you be the lady of the house? You can't be Leah."

"I am Lady Levanah Falcon." She touched fingertips briefly. "This is my aunt, Mrs. Leah Simmons."

"It *is* Price," Leah whispered.

"I was named after my grandfather, ma'am. He came from Kingsmead in Marie Regina. When I was a boy he used to talk about his sister, Leah, and the rest of the family. He used to say sometimes that he'd surprise the family with a letter, but he never did get around to it."

"Is Price—is he dead then?" Leah's hand went to her throat.

"A couple of years back, ma'am. There was a bad epidemic of flu in our parts, and the old man just took to his bed and didn't get up again."

He had seated himself without invitation, and went on chatting unconcernedly as Molly brought in the coffee.

"I guess I ought to have written first, but I

thought it might be kind of fun to give you a surprise. This is the first time I've ever been in the home country, and I've been impressed, I can tell you. There's good, rich land here and a tradition behind it. Seems like one could put down roots."

"So Price married," Leah said. "I never imagined he would settle down."

"He married a Boer girl, ma'am."

"Oh? You're not suggesting he fought on the opposite side during the war, I hope?" Leah said.

"He was interned by the Boers, so he didn't exactly fight on any side," Price said. "My father, Harry, was born before the war started. He was married at seventeen to a neighbor's daughter and I was the result."

"Are your parents alive?" Levanah poured coffee and handed it to him.

"No, ma'am, my mother died when I was born, and my father was killed in a skirmish with some blacks when I was eight. My grandparents brought me up. The old lady died when I was sixteen. After that it was just the old man and me, and when he went I got a hankering to come over here."

"With your family?" Levanah inquired.

"Oh, I'm not married," Price said. "The truth is I have it in mind to marry a Limey girl, maybe settle here. I made a good profit on the shearing last year, and I left a good man in charge."

"You're a sheep farmer?" Leah said.

"Yes, ma'am. My great-grandparents had a spread and my grandfather took it over."

"I simply cannot imagine my brother herding sheep," Leah said. "He was all for rushing off to find diamonds."

"My grandmother was a pretty strong-minded

woman," Price grinned. "A handsome one too, and she had a nice piece of property as her dowry."

"Is it large?" Levanah inquired.

"Seventy thousand acres, ma'am. A tidy piece."

"Seventy thou—! As you say, a tidy piece."

"If I can find me a wife here," Price confided, "I'll sell off the farm and get something here. I'd like my children to grow up in the old country."

"You'd like children?" Levanah asked.

"Doesn't everybody? I'm close on thirty and it's time I wed. A man can't footloose forever. Anyway, I'd like to hand down what I've got to my own flesh and blood. As things are now, if anything happens to me, I've willed the lot to a cousin of my mother's."

"We will have to look for a wife for you, won't we, Aunt Leah?"

"Hey, that really sounds like something!" he exclaimed. "Aunt Leah in the flesh. Grandpa talked about you a lot. Said you took over the household after his parents died. Very efficient, with a good head on her shoulders, was how he described you. He always said how grateful he was to you for encouraging him to emigrate. He had a couple more sisters, didn't he? Edith and—was it Beth?"

"They're dead," Leah said, and her lips were briefly compressed as if in pain.

"We'd better explain the various members of the family," Levanah said, smoothly, "or you'll be completely confused. Aunt Leah is a widow but she's bringing up her two orphaned granddaughters here at Kingsmead. Sigrid is fourteen and Margot is nearly ten. I am Beth Falcon's daughter, by the way."

"That would be Grandpa's youngest sister?"

"I married my cousin, Teddy. John Falcon's son. He and Edith Falcon's son were killed in the Great War. I was left with twins to rear. Johnny is Lord Falcon, of course. Selena is married to another cousin."

"That's a lot of inbreeding," Price said. "It's not a good thing with sheep."

"Fortunately we are dealing with people," Levanah said crisply. "My son-in-law, Giles Shaw, is a farmer too, not sheep, crops and some dairy stock. He and Selena have a farm at the other side of the river. They are expecting their first child so we are naturally very excited."

"It all sounds a mite confusing," Price said.

"You'll get us all sorted out in time. You will be staying here, of course?"

"I've booked in at that quaint little place in the village," he told them. "I walked over. Makes a nice stroll on a summer day."

"But you must stay with us," Levanah said.

Her eyes were glowing and she looked charming.

"It's very good of you," he said.

"Not in the least. You're family." She rose, the pleats of her black dress spraying about her. "You'll need to have your things sent over, or would you like to borrow the car and run it down? Wait! I'll get the keys."

"It's real generous of you, ma'am." He unfolded his long length and beamed.

"Call me Levanah. We are, after all, second cousins."

She went out with him into the hall and Leah heard them laughing together. The solar was full of sunshine, its warm fingers turning the dark panels to honey. After a little while she heard the car drive away and Levanah came back into the room.

"Don't ever tell me that life is dull again," she said. "Who would have thought that a solution to the problem would arrive literally on the doorstep?"

"Problem?"

"Of Selena and Giles and their wanting to leave."

"He said he had land to sell," Leah recalled. "Do you mean that Giles could buy it? He's never farmed sheep."

"Your mind isn't working very quickly today," Levanah said, irritated. "What possible benefit could it be for Giles to buy a sheep farm? He and Selena would still leave."

"It was a shock," Leah excused herself; "seeing Price's grandson. He is extraordinarily like Price. My brother had exactly the same carefree manner. John was much quieter and reserved."

"Never mind your brothers. They're dead and gone."

"I was very fond of them," Leah said. "We were a happy family once. My mother, Margred, was gay and sweet. She used to sing Welsh songs as she went about the house, and she adored my father. After he died she lost all interest in living. It was as if she just waited to rejoin him."

"Will you stop meandering and *listen*!" Levanah demanded. "This house can be a happy one again with Falcon children to live in it, to carry on the name."

"If Johnny marries"

"He may very well marry but there's no profit in sitting about waiting for him to make up his mind," Levanah said. "And if he dies without sons the next Lord Falcon will be that South African."

"He said he was going to take an English wife."

"And when he does, and if anything happened to Johnny, he could come in here and turn us all out like as not. He'd be the new Lord Falcon and the estate is entailed. I've been sent away from here once but I'll not have it happen again."

"I've lived my whole life here. I'm nearly seventy-five," Leah said, frightened. "I'm too old to be moved."

"Then pay attention! Johnny would never make us leave. He's not very interested in the estate except as a place to visit when he needs a change of air. But he's reckless, like his father was, and he might not make old bones. In that case Price would inherit. Now, if Price were to marry Selena, she's my own daughter and she'd never dream of making us go."

"But Selena is married to Giles."

"That can be arranged."

"Oh, not divorce!" Leah exclaimed. "Divorce always causes such an ugly scandal."

"If Giles were to die, quite soon," her niece said softly.

"He's very healthy. It would have to be an accident."

"Not another car crash." Levanah sat, drumming her fingers, her brow creased.

"What then?"

"I have it." Levanah smiled gently. "He is going over to Maidstone next week to take a delivery of a new combine harvester. If anything were to go wrong with it while he was testing it—poor Selena, only three months gone, and a widow. And Price Falcon looking for a nice bit of land and an English wife."

"Selena would inherit Whittle Farm," Leah said.

"They would both be on the spot if anything were to happen to Johnny. I do believe," said Levanah, "in taking out a little insurance."

Price Falcon, driving cautiously along the main road, for he was more at ease in the saddle than in the driving seat, admired the trim green hedges and lush meadows that stretched on both sides. This, he thought, was the England of which his grandfather had talked so nostalgically. He had loved his grandfather in a hearty, uncomplicated way, had striven to imitate the old man's clipped English way of talking, had listened eagerly to tales of the other's youth.

"The Gaiety Girls! Ah, there were some high-steppers! Not that I stood a chance with 'em. They wouldn't look at anything lower than an earl. But I had my own little filly. Grace her name was. Grace Finn. Red hair and the bluest eyes you ever saw. Common as dirt, of course. I gave her up—can't remember why now. She bored me probably. But I can still see that red hair."

His grandfather chuckling at his memories, and a girl with curly red hair sauntering out of a gate. He pulled up and leaned over to open the other door, inquiring, "Good day! Would you like a lift?"

"I'd like to know what you're doing in my mother's car," she retorted.

"Hey! Then you must be Selena! Johnny Falcon's sister?"

"And who are you?" Gray eyes in a distractingly pretty face surveyed him.

"Do get in. It's quite safe. I'm not a desperado, just a long-lost cousin. The name's Price Falcon."

She joined him in the car, her face puzzled. "Price? Aunt Leah had a brother once—"

"Who went to South Africa. I'm his grandson."

"So it really does happen like that sometimes!" She laughed, her short nose crinkling. "I mean the long-lost cousin arriving—do you own a diamond mine?"

"A sheep farm, but I'm thinking of selling up."

"And Giles is thinking of going out to Australia to farm there for a few years. We're just waiting until after the baby is born."

There was a wedding ring on her finger and a very faint bulge under her dress.

"Giles is your husband?"

"Nobody else's," she said gaily. "We live at Whittle Farm. It's hidden from here by the ruins."

"Is that the old monastery?" he inquired.

"Oh, it was one hundreds of years ago," Selena said. "King Henry the Eighth threw the monks out and some of my ancestors grabbed a lot of the land. Aunt Leah knows more about all that than I do."

"Where shall I drop you?" he asked.

"In the village if you're going that way. I promised Wenna—that's my mother-in-law—to pick up some wool. She's knitting like fury for her first grandchild."

"And what were you doing in the field?" he asked curiously.

"I was wandering about," she said demurely, "and thinking beautiful thoughts. You know it's said to be very important for an unborn child to be surrounded by peace and music and flowers. So I wander off and—think beautiful thoughts!"

She laughed again and a pang of regret struck him as the sun flashed on her wedding ring.

"Are you staying in the village?" she inquired. "I planned to, but Lady Levanah—*Cousin*, I suppose I can say—very kindly asked me if I'd put up at Kingsmead."

"Oh." As he turned the car down the steep incline which led to the village, she gave him a quick undecided glance.

"It was all right for me to accept, wasn't it? I haven't broken any unwritten laws, have I?"

"Of course not. It's only that—Kingsmead is a bit gloomy," she said hesitantly. "Johnny and I never liked the house much, even when we were children. It's creepy."

"It's very old."

"So is Whittle Farm, but it's not creepy."

They had drawn up in front of the inn, and she broke off to put her head through the window and call, "Sigrid! Margot! Come over here and meet a cousin from South Africa."

Two children, who were sitting on the churchyard wall, jumped down and crossed the green. Price, getting out of his car, found himself looking down into two identical round faces, the one surmounted by flaxen braids, the other with brown plaits. The elder of the two, the blonde, gave a jerky little nod and said, "How do you do? I am Sigrid von Braun. This is my sister, Margot. She is nearly ten and I am fourteen. What sort of cousin are you?"

"A distant one, I suppose. My grandfather was your grandmother's brother."

"That would be Price," said Sigrid. "The one who went to South Africa. Leah told us about him."

"You call your grandmother by her Christian name?" He felt a trifle shocked.

"Sometimes we call her Grandmother and sometimes we call her Aunt Leah like Cousin Levanah does. It's not important," said the blond girl.

"What's your name?" Margot asked.

"Price. Price Falcon." He had the impression of being measured and cast aside.

"I shall call you Cousin Price," said Sigrid.

"So shall I." Margot nodded gravely, her small brown eyes regarding him steadily.

"Well, that's fine." There was no reason for it but he felt chilly though no wind had violated the sunshine.

"You will be staying at Kingsmead?" asked Sigrid. "If you're family, they'll want that."

"Who?"

"Leah and Levanah," Margot said. "They like family to stay in the big house. Selena won't."

"As you see, I escaped," Selena said lightly. "Did you leave your luggage here?"

"We'll get it for you," said Margot.

"And put it in the car and ride back with you," Sigrid added.

They turned and went sedately into the inn.

"Monsters, aren't they?" Selena said. There was a little frown on her pretty face.

"They're—unusual," he said.

"We're an unusual family." She gave a bleak little smile. "If you feel the need for company drive over to the farm. I'd like to have you meet my husband."

"Thanks, I will." Again he was seized by a pang of regret and an uneasiness impossible to define.

Chapter 15

"Such a beautiful harvest!" Wenna cried. "I never saw the world so green and golden."

"I thought we might have a picnic," Michael hinted.

"And you can continue the painting you began." She smiled across at him affectionately. His eyes were not now good enough for close line work or etching, but he derived great pleasure from oils, slapping on the color in great swathes of thick primitive vitality.

"I shall be glad," she said, "when a teacher is found. The flat is too cramped, and the children are becoming impossible to handle."

"You reared your own well."

"More than twenty years ago. I was younger then, and in any case I could not have done it without your help. But as soon as Levanah finds someone suitable I shall go back to the farm with no regrets."

"You will miss Giles and Selena," he said.

She was silent for a moment, considering. When she raised her head her face was serious.

"I'll miss them enormously but it's better for them to go away for a while," she said slowly. "I am not happy, Michael. Ever since that young man arrived—"

"He's a very pleasant young man."

"I know that, and he's fitted into the family as if he'd been born and bred here. A fortnight only and he is on first-name terms with everyone in the district."

"Then what troubles you?"

"It is Selena," Wenna said. "Price admires her very greatly."

"She's a lovely girl.'

"I know. Lovely and high-spirited and lively. She and Johnny are their father all over again, just as Giles has Cal's love of the land in his blood. Selena is flattered by Price's little gallantries."

"Surely they're harmless enough," he argued mildly.

"If they remain so, but no relationship can stand still. It must either grow or die. And Giles spends so much of his time poring over livestock catalogues and fiddling with tractors that he is apt to forget that wives need a little attention too. Why, he's off in the south meadow today, playing with the new harvester."

"My dear, you worry too much."

"Which means you want to change the subject before it begins to bore you. You're a transparent man, Michael!"

"A fortunate one," he said and caught at her hand as she rose.

At two years short of seventy she had grown into

old age with the ease of an acorn maturing into a tree. She had put on a little weight but it suited her, and her white hair was as plentiful as ever. In her face humor and serenity mingled, and her eyes had lost none of their green.

"I still think I'm right," she said stubbornly. "It will be wiser for Giles and Selena to go away for a time after the baby is born. Shall I make some sandwiches and get out the car?"

"Where is Selena now?"

"At home, I suppose. Or sitting in the wheat 'thinking beautiful thoughts.' Such nonsense. I carried my child without having heard of any of these newfangled theories."

"I believe the ancient Egyptians surrounded pregnant women with beautiful objects and played soothing music to them," he said.

Wenna's sniff demonstrated her opinion of the ancient Egyptians.

At Whittle Farm Selena rested her feet on the sofa and tried to pay attention to her book. It was, however, an exceedingly dull plot and her glance kept wandering toward the window. Price had told her that he would look in during the course of the afternoon. She would have preferred Giles to sit with her, but he always seemed to be busy these days, and it was weeks since he had taken her out anywhere. Price at least looked at her as if she were still a person and not merely the woman who was going to have a baby. Price was amusing too. She loved hearing him talk about his farm on the veldt where the stars hung low over sun-yellowed grass and the native Kaffirs built fires that leaped toward the sky.

"You should go to South Africa, not Australia," he

had said. "Why not take a lease on my property and put me in here as manager while you're gone?"

"Giles has his heart set on Australia," Selena said.

"And you'll not dissuade him? I thought in this family the women ruled the roost!"

"I'm a Shaw now and in *my* family the husband takes the lead."

Thinking back over that statement now she feared it sounded docile and dull. Perhaps she was becoming dull. Giles had recently got into the habit of patting her on the backside and calling her "old girl." Old girl!

She tossed the book aside and went over to the mirror, peering anxiously into it. Her face looked rounder than usual and she had not bothered recently to put lemon juice on her freckles. She looked, she decided, plump, placid and pregnant! No wonder Giles spent more time in the fields than with her. He was in the south meadow this very minute, trying out the new harvester. Instead of waiting in for Price she'd walk over to see Giles. He and the other men might be glad of some cold beer on such a hot day. Imperceptibly her spirits lifted as she hunted for a wide-brimmed hat.

"Concentrate," said Levanah, her voice a tense whisper in the green darkness of the cottage. "Draw down the power. Invoke the Destroyer."

Always the destroyer, Leah thought. *Even in grain time she thinks only of destruction.*

I wish we came here at night, Sigrid thought. *We always used to, before Price came. I don't like Price. I don't understand why Levanah makes such a fuss of him, nor why she keeps pushing him at Selena. Selena has a husband already.*

I wonder who is going to be dead, Margot thought. *I wish I could be there to watch, instead of here*.

"Invoke," Levanah urged, and she raised her arms high and chanted low, over and over.

"Kali, Kali, Kali, Kali, Kali."

The whitewashed walls and the shuttered windows caught and held the words.

Price, having walked over from Kingsmead, slowed his stride as he approached the farm. The warm bright afternoon had refreshed him. It was only as that idea occurred to him that he realized he had been feeling jaded. It was not anything physical, more a general malaise of spirits for which he was quite unable to account.

Kingsmead was the most beautiful house he had ever entered, and the Falcons could not have been more hospitable. Johnny he had not yet met, but Selena was exactly the wife he would have chosen for himself. Giles was a good fellow too, and his mother and stepfather a pair of old dears. But those people were not, to his way of reckoning, the main family.

The main family lived at Kingsmead and consisted of the four around whom the life of the great house revolved. The two girls he disliked in a vague and embarrassed way, for they had done nothing to merit it. They were unusually polite schoolchildren, never quarreling or arguing, always together with their hair neatly braided and their clothes clean. Yet whenever he saw them with their smiling mouths and watching eyes he felt uneasy.

"Don't you play with other girls?" he had asked.

"We don't like other girls," Sigrid said.

"And they don't like us very much," added Margot.

She had not spoken sadly, but with a curious glee, and she and her sister had glanced at each other as if they shared something very amusing.

Levanah and Leah had gone out of their way to make him feel part of the family. They too were almost always together, but there was no feeling of closeness between them though they spoke sweetly, each seeming greatly concerned for the other's welfare. And Levanah fascinated him. With her flawless white skin and slim figure it was difficult to believe she was in her mid-forties. Everything about her was of cool, understated elegance, from her smooth hair to the black shoes with their pointed toes and curved heels. She was, he thought, a lovely woman in an odd, fey style. It was strange that since her husband's death she had chosen to bury herself on this country estate.

When he said as much she had laughed.

"The estate and I go together," she told him. "Did your grandfather not tell you about the witch woman who came from Wales long ago to wed a Falcon? She bore the devil's kiss on her thigh in the shape of a crescent moon, and she passed on the mark to certain of her female descendants. And those who carry the mark always live at Kingsmead."

He had wanted to ask if she had the mark herself, and she had divined his wish and said smiling, "After me there is nobody who carries the mark. So you see Kingsmead and I go together. And Aunt Leah would be very upset if I were to marry again. She is devoted to the memory of my late husband, as I am."

He had not argued but had privately thought that it was a pity Johnny didn't come home more often, as a little masculine influence in the house might inject some new life into the peaceful, woman-dominated routine. And, having thought of the adjective "peaceful," his mind rejected the word. Beneath the surface calm of the ancient house something brooded.

He shook off his imaginings and turned in, not at the main gate, but at the side gate that gave access to the south meadows. Its acres had been devoted to wheat and the golden fronds feathered the blue air. On the crest of the field he could see the new harvester with the tiny figure of Giles perched aloft. He waved, but the other was too distant to see him, so he began to walk in that direction, his head bent to the yellow stems of wheat and the occasional red face of an intruding poppy.

Levanah was circling against the way of the sun, her eyes wide open and gleaming, her thin fingers curved. She chanted still in a monotone, her voice forming sounds rather than words. In her mind Giles Shaw grew sleepy, his eyes closing, his thoughts blurring, his head drooping. She willed sleep into his mind, willed oblivion into his thoughts.

Behind her the others circled too, their hands upstretched to catch the power, their minds emptied of everything but the thought of death.

Giles, beginning the long descent of the curving hill, shook his head slightly as he turned in his seat to check the accuracy of the wide swath the harvester was cutting. He felt unaccountably sleepy, the result possibly of working too long in the hot sun. When he had finished this section he'd take a break and go back to the farm for a snack and a cool drink.

Selena would be pleased if he spent a little time with her. He'd neglected her recently, and his mother had already hinted, none too subtly, that neglected wives, like cows, were apt to stray.

"I see a field," said Cat. "I see a wheat field. A young man on a tractor of some kind but higher and bigger with rotating blades. There is a young woman with a heavy basket in each hand. Bottles of something, very heavy. She is stopping to rest, sitting down in the wheat. There are poppies growing near her. She is putting out her hand to pluck one. That wheat is above her head as she sits there."

"What else can you see?" Leone asked.

It had been many months since Cat had had a seeing time. She had never confided in the older woman her reason for coming back from London without going on into Kent. That she had undergone some traumatic experience was obvious, but as she volunteered no information Leone respected her privacy.

"I can see another man, also crossing the field," Cat said. "He is looking at the ground. Now he is looking up. The machine—whatever it is—is coming faster down the hill. The man on it is looking back and shaking his head. He seems confused, sleepy. The machine is going much faster. The other man has begun to run toward the young woman. He is shouting and waving his arms about. The young woman is beginning to look around, beginning to rise. There is a mist of sleep about the man's head. Black sleep, heavy, heavy."

"What is it? Cat, what is it?" Leone cried.

"It's evil," the younger woman shuddered. "Blood

and screaming and crunching of bone and slicing of flesh, and a chaos turning the day dark."

"Come back. Don't get involved."

Cat shivered, her eyes focusing again upon the kitchen. Between the coils of black hair her face was chalk-white, her lips trembling.

"Are you all right?"

Leone rose and poured a cup of tea.

"Yes. Yes, I'm fine. I didn't see what happened in the end. It was muddled and confused. Thanks."

She cupped the hot drink between her hands and sipped gratefully. After a moment she raised her head and said quietly, "I have to go to Kingsmead as soon as possible. I've waited too long already, and now something in me tells me that I have to go."

"Are you certain?"

Cat nodded, her face thoughtful.

"That London newspaper where you saw the advertisement—do you still have it?"

"It's here, on the dresser. You said you weren't interested."

"I am now." Cat took the paper and read the circled item.

" 'Wanted. Young lady to teach general subjects to junior pupils at small private school. No previous experience necessary, but a high educational standard and a sympathetic, pleasant nature essential. Generous salary and furnished, rent-free accommodation. Apply Lady Levanah Falcon, Kingsmead, Marie Regina, Kent.' "

"By now someone may have been engaged."

"I don't think so. I was meant to see the advertisement, meant to see what I saw just now. It was the sign."

"Do you want to go?"

Cat shook her head. Her voice, as she replied, held an infinity of sadness.

"All my life I wanted to meet my mother, to see the big house and the white cottage. Now I don't want to leave Saron. I don't want to go into Kent, but I have to go. The time has come for me to set things right. I don't know how or why, but I have to do it."

"Will you go alone?" Leone asked.

"I have to," said Cat. "I have to do everything alone. I know it without knowing why."

In the blood-spattered wheat Selena stood, her eyes saucered in horror, her mouth rounded into what should have been a scream but emerged as a series of whimpers.

They were towing away the wrecked harvester. An ambulance had just removed a covered stretcher. Giles, his face bruised and cut where he had flung himself upon the brake in a last, desperate attempt to check the speed, was by her side. Words poured from him tonelessly.

"The brakes failed, and I was tired. I was so tired that my eyes were closing. I couldn't stop it. He ran right in front of it. It was to warn you, I think. It was to warn you to get out of the way. I couldn't avoid him and I couldn't stop. At the last moment he stumbled and fell."

"I have a pain," Selena said in a high shrill voice, and bent double suddenly, moaning. "Oh God, I have a terrible pain!"

He was jolted out of shock into terrified concern as she sank to her knees, her face twisted with pain.

"I don't understand it," Levanah was saying, as she paced restlessly up and down the long drawing room. "I don't understand what went wrong. I don't understand how it happened."

"It was an accident," Leah said.

"They are *all* accidents!" her niece said angrily. "We work upon the mind, as you well know. And Giles was going to sleep! It was Giles who ought to have died. Why that fool had to run in front at the last moment—"

"Selena was in the path of the harvester below the level of the wheat."

"And Price was being gallant! Much use it was as she's lost the baby anyway," Levanah said savagely.

"She is going to recover?"

"Oh, she's young and healthy. She's capable of having a dozen babies. Shaw babies!" Levanah said in disgust.

"We cannot provide for every eventuality," Leah said.

"But we should render the margin of error as narrow as possible. I ought to have guarded against intrusion."

"And now?" Leah's voice was fearful.

"We have to get Johnny married. All he thinks about are those wretched airplanes he is learning to fly. His latest is called a Tiger Moth, if you please, and he's promising to 'take a spin in our direction,' as he puts it. He will be home for Easter, he says. I only hope the new teacher is young and lovely, but from the replies I've had so far all the applicants seem to be past forty. But I have to drive back to Whittle Farm now. Wenna is breaking the news gently to Michael, so somebody has to organize Giles."

"Will there be an inquest?"

"A formality." Levanah was shrugging on her coat. "The brakes failed. Giles was overcome by the heat. Price died a hero. Aunt, I have to go—I only came back to tell you what had happened."

"If we had come back from the cottage along the main road instead of through the woods, we'd have seen all the people running."

"And probably said something that would have roused suspicion. You show your feelings too transparently. Where are the girls?"

"Out somewhere." Leah's tone was abstracted.

"If they come in see that they get a good supper. I'll see you tomorrow probably."

Levanah's heels tapped briskly through the French windows. Leah rose and walked beneath the curved arch with its heavy apricot brocade curtain into the old wing where parlor and solar were divided by double doors.

Her usual place on the low sill was occupied by a newspaper with a crossword puzzle partly filled in. Price had been working on it that morning. In this very room half a century before she had encouraged his grandfather to evade his gambling debts by leaving the country. Time had run round in a circle.

"Widdershins," said Leah aloud, and began to weep the painful wracking tears of a soul that has forgotten the meaning of remorse.

"There's nothing much to see," Margot said in disappointment, staring at the smashed and trampled wheat.

"The police took everything away," Sigrid reminded her.

"Selena was taken to the hospital at Maidstone."

"But she lost the baby right here," Sigrid said. "It came out of her in bits and pieces. I heard Greta Stone talking about it."

"Selena's baby came *out* in bits and pieces, and Cousin Price went *in* in bits and pieces," Margot giggled.

"There might be some blood somewhere," Sigrid said. "Oh no, it's only a poppy."

"I didn't like Cousin Price," Margot said thoughtfully, "but I didn't think he'd die."

"I think something went wrong," said Sigrid. "Levanah was angry."

"Girls! Girls, come here at once." Wenna was calling them from the gate.

They composed their faces and walked sedately toward her.

"You ought to be at home," Wenna scolded.

"We came up to see if we could help," Sigrid said.

"It's not helping anybody to stand there indulging your morbid curiosity," Wenna said sharply. "Cousin Levanah has offered to stay over at the farm with Giles and I am going back to Michael. This has been a great shock to him."

"Is he going to die too?" Margot asked brightly.

"Nobody else is going to die," Wenna said firmly. "Now you must go home or your grandmother will begin to worry. She has had a great shock too."

"I think you and Michael will live for a long time yet," Sigrid murmured. "Levanah is so very fond of you both. Come on, Margot."

As they came through the gate and began to walk up the road, Wenna had a cold, sick feeling.

"Delayed shock," she whispered aloud, but her gaze was fixed on the two retreating figures. The sun was sinking rapidly and a grayness was stealing over the landscape. The children's shadows were scarcely discernible.

It was quite natural for healthy children to take an interest in the more gruesome aspects of death. She had known these particular children all their lives, taught them in school every day, had grieved for their parents. There was no reason in the world for her to feel this creeping horror.

Giles had wanted to stay with Selena, but the doctors had persuaded him to return home. He had blamed himself over and over, and finally given way to an outburst of sobbing such as she had not witnessed in him since his childhood.

"God forgive me," she said aloud, as she began to walk slowly toward the school. "God forgive me, but those two children have something about them that chills my blood."

She tried to pray for them both, with no clear idea as to why they should need her prayers, but the words jumbled in her mind and her head ached and for the first time she felt old and afraid.

Against her will she found herself saying, "Lord, defend us from the powers of darkness."

Chapter 16

"So you are Catherine Beck? I hope you had a comfortable journey."

Levanah shook hands cordially as she spoke, and motioned the young woman to a chair by the fire.

"Thank you, yes."

"But a long one, all the way from Wales. The Falcons have Welsh blood in them. Originally some of them came from just outside Caernarvon."

"I'm from Wrexham," Cat said. She had posted her letter of application from there.

"You say you have a good school certificate—no, there's no need to produce it. I consider personality to be more important than mere academic qualifications. I also pride myself on being an excellent judge of character. You have not taught before, you said?"

"No, Lady Levanah. It has not been necessary for me to earn my living before this."

Levanah studied the newcomer. Small and wiry, skin tanned, black hair drawn back severely into a bun, beautiful slanting green eyes, dowdy clothes. Of respectable family, judging by her manner and her handwriting in the letter she had sent. Her bone structure was delicate, but she had made no attempt to improve herself with cosmetics or perfumes. Yet it was possible that Johnny, when he came home, would be attracted by subtlety.

"You said you were fond of children," she prompted.

"Yes. Yes, I like children."

"You will have twenty pupils under the age of twelve, apart from my cousin. Sigrid is nearly fifteen, but rather than send her away to school or make the long drive into Maidstone every day, we preferred her to stay on at the Manor School. You will find she is a help with the little ones, and she works alone very competently without the need for much supervision. Her younger sister, Margot, also attends the school."

Levanah went on smoothly, discussing salary, holidays, timetables. The young woman sat, apparently listening, but she had an odd withdrawn look in her eyes as if she were listening to something quite different. Her hands were clasped so tightly together that the knuckles showed white.

"The school stands on the site of an ancient manor house which was part of the estate," Levanah said. "My aunt, Mrs. Leah Simmons, founded the school in memory of my grandmother, Lady Margred. For the past two years or so a distant cousin of ours, Mrs. Shaw, has been teaching there, but she is past retiring age. Indeed she only stayed on until Christmas as you were due to come in the new year. Are you feeling quite well, Miss Beck?"

"I am a little tired," Cat said. "This is a very old house too, isn't it?"

"It was built in 1536," Levanah said. "We are planning a small family celebration next month to mark the anniversary. But you'd like some tea, I'm sure."

"I had something on the train." Cat could not tear her eyes from the pale, flawless face of the woman who had given birth to her and abandoned her so many years before. This situation had occurred so often in her imagination that the reality itself lacked substance.

"Oh, and here is Aunt Leah."

Levanah had risen and was smiling in the direction of the wide stone staircase. An old woman, white-haired, slightly bent, was coming down.

"Aunt Leah, our new teacher, Miss Beck, has just arrived. Miss Beck, this is my aunt, Mrs. Simmons."

They shook hands. Leah had dark eyes, heavy-lidded with gleams of brightness still flashing from their depths. Her lined skin had a yellowish tinge and her hand was clawlike.

"We are very pleased you were able to come," she said. "Not many young teachers wish to bury themselves in such a small village."

"I like the country," Cat said.

"Because you think it's peaceful?" Leah gave an odd rasping laugh. "Terrible things can happen here. Last autumn a great-nephew of mine, who was visiting here from South Africa, was killed when he fell beneath a combine harvester."

"How dreadful!"

"Far too dreadful to serve as a topic for conversation," Levanah said. "Miss Beck looks quite sick."

"I would really like to get down to the school," Cat said.

"Of course you would, to explore while it's still light. How wise of you to arrive in the early afternoon."

"I stayed overnight in London," Cat said.

"I go up to town as seldom as possible," Levanah said. "I heartily dislike the smoke and noise, and I really don't care to leave my dear aunt too long alone. Since my husband's death she and I have been inseparable."

"Yes, indeed," Leah said. Her voice was suddenly flat and dull.

"You don't drive? Then I'll run you over to the school now. You did take all your luggage out of the taxi."

"I've only the two cases."

"Then we'll drive down," Levanah said.

As they moved toward the main door, Leah said, "That young woman reminds me of somebody and I can't think who it is."

"My aunt is sometimes a trifle muddled in her mind," Levanah said as they went out into the courtyard. "Of course she is in her mid-seventies but my father is in his ninety-sixth year and exceedingly alert. He is Michael Shaw, the artist. Perhaps you've heard of him?"

"Yes. He's very well known."

They had passed under the arch into the tree-lined avenue, where a car was parked. The wind was a bitter January one, tossing the remaining leaves.

"You'll find we're rather a complicated family," Levanah said, ushering Cat into the passenger seat. "I was married to my cousin. My son, the present Lord Falcon, is not married, but my daughter married *her* cousin. She and Giles live at Whittle Farm, but they plan to emigrate soon. Giles is the son of Cousin Wenna—"

"Who taught at the school?"

"And was married to yet another cousin. To complicate matters further, when she was a middle-aged widow, she married my own father, Michael Shaw. They moved back to Whittle Farm with Giles and Selena when the school closed for the Christmas holidays, so the flat is empty now. I did stock it with groceries yesterday and you need only take a short walk into the village. This bridge spans the river and Marie Regina proper is down in the hollow. Whittle Farm is beyond the hill, and this is the entrance to the school."

The great house she had recognized from her seeing times, but the building before her was unfamiliar. It was set in the midst of a rather shabby lawn at which her employer cast a disparaging glance as they got out of the car.

"The children run about so much on it in term time that the turf never gets the chance to recover," she said. "Well, you have a week in which to settle down before the new term begins. Shall I come in with you or do you prefer to sniff the atmosphere alone? For myself I always hated guided tours! I believe some families are beginning to open their homes for public viewing. Can you imagine anything more ghastly!"

Flippant, smart as paint in a sable-collared black suit, her eyes as yellow as amber caught in sunlight, the black pearl on her left hand throbbing with power. *And this*, thought Cat, waving automatically as the car described an arc on the gravel, *is my mother. Johnny's mother too. Darling, darling*

Johnny. I wish that thinking about him didn't hurt so much. If he comes home to Kingsmead—dear God, what shall I say or do?

The front door was unlocked. She put her two suitcases into the narrow passage and straightened. A flight of stairs lay ahead, but some compulsion was urging her to go outside again. The back of her nose was itching violently and a jumble of pictures flashed through her mind. The girl in the portrait, with bleeding wrists. The man drowsily nodding on the high seat of what looked like a big tractor. A small white house.

She began to walk rapidly back down the drive onto the main road. Opposite the ruin-crowned hill rose sharply. On her right the river thrashed beneath the bridge, and on its farther bank trees tangled to the water's edge. In this cultivated landscape only the wood was ungroomed and wanton. Reason and intuition drove her across the bridge and down the steeply twisting path into the crowding trunks. Their branches laced and weaved above her head and the brambles set traps for her ankles, but the path, though ill-defined, was there. She followed its twists and turns, and came into a clearing. The word was not perhaps the right one to describe it, for the grass had been spared scythe or mower for many a long year, and creepers almost smothered the whitewashed cottage with its shuttered windows.

She went up to the front door and stared at it thoughtfully. In her waking dream her grandmother had stood here with a lost look in her eyes. The door was locked, and for a moment she was tempted to go away again. She was, after all, trespassing. Then she spotted the loose stone in the step, almost impercepti-ble had her shoe not caught against it, wobbling it slightly. The key was under the stone—a spare key, she guessed, so that those who used the place could slip in whenever they felt like it. She fitted the key into the lock, noting that it turned easily and that the door itself swung inward silently.

It opened into a living room with a few pieces of old, beautifully carved furniture, a couple of rugs, a tapestry frame, cups and saucers ranged on the narrow shelves of a dresser. The atmosphere was peaceful and friendly. The remains of a fire were in the grate and the place had evidently been dusted.

It was dim even with the light from the open door, and the bolts of the shutters were rusted into their sockets, but there were candles on the table. She fumbled in her pocket for matches and lit one.

Narrow wooden stairs led up out of the living room, and the door at the foot of them was closed. Staring at the door she was conscious of more than a physical barrier. A darkness barred her way so intensely that the candlestick shook with the trembling of her hand.

So the evil was concentrated in that room, and it was a present evil, not the memory of deeds long done. She drew the moonstone ring from the chain about her neck and slipped it into place on the forefinger of her right hand. There was a cross on the chain. Leone had given it to her for her twenty-first birthday. Now she let it hang outside her coat, where it glittered bravely against the dark cloth.

For a few moments she stood motionless, her head bowed, her lips moving in the ancient words of protection against evil. Then she picked up the candle again and went steadily forward to open the door.

The room was still clouded by the fumes of incense, and a red lamp glowed on the wide shelf under

the horned mask. She stared at the low table with the
bones laid out upon it, the four chairs draped with
the black robes, the carved sword with its deeply cut
symbols. Against the farther wall shelves reached up
to the ceiling. She walked over and looked at the objects on them. Shudders of disgust wracked her
slight frame and vomit stung her throat. The dark
and sinister aspects of the craft she and Leone had
practiced together for ten years rose up in the fore-
front of her mind. Leone had taught her how to deal
with these abominations, but she had never seen any
so vile, and for an instant her heart quailed at the
magnitude of the task. Then she reminded herself
that these things in themselves were harmless. It was
the intention behind them and the uses to which
they were put that rendered them malign.

She looked around for a moment more and saw
then what she was seeking. Four cups occupied the
surface of a small table, each cup marked with a
name. She read the names. Leah. Levanah. Sigrid.
Margot. The four who came here by dark of the
moon to drink blasphemy and weave the bloody
strands of unnatural destiny. These were the four
with whom she must deal. She felt for a moment
small and afraid and inadequate. Then she went
swiftly back into the other room closing the door behind her, blew out the candle as she replaced it on
the table, and left the cottage. As she knelt to put the
key under the step the impression that she was not
alone came over her so strongly that she looked up
nervously at the shuttered windows. It was as if the
house itself were watching her. It was, she thought,
a charming little place where loving people should be
happy, not a place where evil was invoked behind
locked doors.

She reached the main road again without seeing anybody, recrossed the bridge and went swiftly up the drive. Before she could do whatever needed to be done there were her clothes to unpack, the flat to explore, the practical details of her new life to be thought out. She put her fears into another part of her mind and began to carry her suitcases up the stairs.

It was past midnight when she had finished sorting through the books in the big classroom. The prospect of teaching bothered her very little. It would, she imagined, be easy enough to make lessons interesting for her pupils. The most important part of her mission in Marie Regina was not to teach, but to bind.

She locked the door of the big sitting room and drew the heavy curtains across the windows. Then she began to cast the circle, to mold four little waxen figures and to bind them with thin cords of black silk. As her fingers worked, her lips moved in the low and ancient chant which Leone had taught her. The circle glowed, repelling darkness, and the flames of the candles were hands joined in prayer.

"Bind them from doing evil. Bind them from willing evil. Bind them in the name of Jahweh. Bind them with the chains of impotence under the guardianship of Uriel. Bind them with the waters of inertia under the guardianship of Gabriel. Bind them with the air of confusion under the guardianship of Raphael. Bind them with the steel of unsatisfied evil under the guardianship of Michael. Bind Leah. Bind Levanah. Bind Sigrid. Bind Margot. Bind!"

Her voice rose and fell with the candle flames and down by the river the long grass parted and sprang

upright again as if unseen creatures moved through it
in solemn procession.

At Kingsmead Leah sat by the window of the solar
and looked out into the darkened courtyard. It was
late but as she grew older she needed less sleep, and
there were nights now when she didn't sleep at all
but sat up until near dawn fearful of closing her eyes
for what the darkness might bring.

The great house was still, though she knew the
stillness was only an illusion and that under the surface, built into the very fabric of the walls, old
griefs and hatreds jostled for attention. There had
been love too but she could no longer remember it.
Yet she had been fond of Levanah once, had taken
pride in treating her in exactly the same way as she
treated her own daughter. Indeed Levanah had always had more freedom than Mary, and had abused
it shamefully. Anger smouldered in Leah's bitter
heart, and with the anger came a slow and deadly
determination. As Leah had suffered so Levanah
would suffer.

I will see her die, the old woman thought, *and as
she dies she will know that in the final reckoning
nothing she has done has been of any value to her.*

The windowpanes were frosted with moonlight
and the creeper that twined up the walls gleamed silver. The fire had burned low and she had not bothered to put on the light. The gloom of the solar was a
protection, for in this room she shrank again behind
the walls of childhood. The darkness of the great hall
was a different matter. There were no electric lights
there to banish the gloom, only the branched candle-
sticks that cast twisted reflections against the walls
and up the wide staircase to the gallery.

She huddled closer to the window, pulling her

black shawl about her shoulders, the weight of her hair heavy in the nape of her neck. Her eyelids prickled with sleep and her hands were aching, so tightly were they pressed together in her lap.

In the bedroom they shared Sigrid and Margot lay wakeful though they had no idea what had roused them. Sigrid thought she had been dreaming, but when she glanced at the other bed she saw that Margot was propped up on her elbow.

"Is something wrong?" she hissed.

"I'm not certain. I feel funny inside," Margot hissed back.

"So do I." The elder girl pulled herself into a sitting position and clasped her knees. "I feel uneasy."

"I had a dream," Margot said. "I dreamed of a tree. A tree with red leaves and a smell like vinegar."

"There used to be a tree like that outside the courtyard," Sigrid said. "It was planted by one of the first Falcon witches and cursed by her. Later on it fell down and killed someone. Grandmother told me about it once."

"She tells interesting stories," Margot approved. "Much better than Wenna. I wonder if the new teacher will tell good stories."

"Levanah said she'd arrived this afternoon," Sigrid mused. "I thought of going over to the school to see her, but Levanah said she'd probably want some time to herself to settle in. Anyway we'll see her soon enough."

"I don't like her," said Margot.

Sigrid aimed a withering look through the darkness.

"That's silly! You've not even met her."

"When I meet her I'll not like her even more,"

the child said calmly. "I may even hate her very much, I've not decided yet."

"We'll have to wait and see." Sigrid yawned and lay down again.

"I don't want to wait," Margot said. "I want to hurt her before she can hurt us. I have a funny feeling about her."

"We'll have to wait and see," Sigrid repeated. Sleep had begun to weigh down her eyelids again and she was disinclined for talk. But Margot went on frowning into the dark, moving her small shoulders irritably as if some burden troubled them.

"Conscience bothering you, Aunt dear?" Levanah had glided, ghost-like, to the door of the solar.

"I was not tired," Leah said wearily. "Go away and let me alone."

"Why, Aunt, I'd never dream of intruding on your privacy," Levanah said sweetly. "I merely wondered if you needed anything. Tea?"

"Only to be let alone," said Leah.

"Certainly. I'll leave you to your memories—then."

She received no answer and, having waited for a moment, said with gentle malice, "It must be comforting to be old and be able to look back. Good night. If you need me I'm never very far away."

In the great hall she took up a candle and stood for a few minutes, her eyes moving slowly round the apartment. Many women must have stood in this place, looking round in despair or satisfaction. She cared nothing now for their joys or sorrows, feeling only a vague respect for those who had, as she had, conquered their circumstances. From being what she termed in her own mind a bastard reared on charity she had become virtual mistress of Kingsmead. The house and its lands were hers to hold in trust for

Johnny. If he came home soon she would make certain that Miss Beck was invited over. The young woman struck her as interesting in a way difficult to define. Certainly it would not be too difficult to gain her confidence and gratitude, and if Johnny were to take a fancy to her—Levanah smiled to herself, picturing a docile daughter-in-law.

A draft blew the flame of her candle sideways and the hall was suddenly an unfamiliar place as if she were seeing it from a completely different angle for the first time. It was a place in which she had no part, and for a moment she was alienated from all that she had fought to possess, and from all that she still hoped to achieve.

She shivered, the cold air striking her neck and arms, tapping icy fingers down her spine. The house was hard to heat despite the abundance of local wood and coal, but she had never realized before how icy it was when the flames had died into ashes and midnight had struck. She began to mount the stairs, walking slowly, without touching the banisters. Leah used a stick now, but Levanah had no intention of allowing age to overtake her.

Ahead of her the portraits of the Falcons were ranged along the wall of the gallery. As a small child she had stood on tiptoe to look at them. Often as she went toward her room their watching eyes had seemed to follow her, to acknowledge her as the heir to their lives, the inheritor of their strange and subtle talents. Their gaze had long since ceased to trouble her. Indeed it had provided a refuge against the occasional doubts that troubled her on the rare occasions when her powers seemed to be weaker than usual. At such times their eyes, following her, had said she had no need to doubt, because in her nature was gathered all the power of their past.

The flame of her candle still wavered and the light that leapt across the painted canvases jerked and twisted. The eyes that had followed and approved her seemed to shift and waver in the changing light. As she turned toward her room she glanced back, caught not by the sense of something watching her, but by the sense of being alone. With a little spasm of terror she saw then that, by what must surely have been some trick of the light, the eyes of the portraits were gazing in the opposite direction as if all her ancestors had decided to ignore her at the same moment.

Epilogue

"Four hundred years is a very long time for one family to live under the same roof," Cat said.

She dropped the remark into a pool of pleasant chatter and sat back to watch the ripples widen. The early part of the evening had been filled with the arrival and departure of neighbors who had accepted the invitation to the buffet meal that marked the anniversary of Kingsmead. There had been cakes and sandwiches and polite conversation and Levanah's smile. Now it was past nine o'clock and the guests had gone, leaving only the immediate family. Cat too had risen to leave, but Levanah held her back.

"Do stay on with the family, Miss Beck. Giles is driving back to Whittle Farm to pick up his parents. Michael gets tired more easily these days and can't endure long social occasions, so he and Wenna are only coming for an hour. You can get a lift back with them when they leave. You must get to know us all better."

"That's very kind of you." Cat had smiled back,

and for an instant something flickered at the back of
Levanah's eyes as if some chord of memory had
struck.

"You live in an old house yourself?" she inquired
now.

"As old as this one, I believe," Cat said, "but very
much smaller of course, and there are only a couple
of acres of land."

"Some of our family's ancestors come from
Wales," Selena remarked. "Not so very far back either. My mother-in-law is Welsh."

"And she was a Falcon cousin," Giles put in. He
and Selena sat together on the sofa that had been
drawn up before one of the twin fireplaces.

Tonight the great hall had a rich and timeless
beauty. Log fires blazed in the hearths and oil lamps
cast their glow on the surfaces of polished wood,
gray tapestry and stone. The long table had been
cleared of dishes save for the decanter and glasses intended for the family toast later. Levanah had
brought in clusters of milky snowdrops and a few
early daffodils and arranged them in crystal bowls
that reflected the sparkling points of light from the
candles set in the enormous chandelier that hung
from the arched and buttressed roof.

Those who sat in the midst of this were, thought
Cat, part of it, showing in their features the blended
characteristics of all those who had lived at
Kingsmead through the centuries. The women wore
evening gowns, Leah and Levanah in their usual
black, Selena in a green dress that flattered her red
curls, the two girls in flowered white dresses with
wide sashes and puffed sleeves. Cat, as befitted the
schoolteacher, wore a long green skirt and a modestly

cut white lace blouse. Yet she too felt at ease in this house where so many had lived and died.

"All their portraits are up there," Giles went on, nodding towards the stairs. "There were a few rogues among them, I daresay. Times are not so colorful now."

"You speak very knowledgeably for someone who has never lived in Kingsmead," Levannah said.

"My father was a Falcon." Giles had flushed angrily.

"On the wrong side of the blanket," Levanah returned sweetly. "Now don't be offended. I was born out of wedlock myself and I rose to be mistress of Kingsmead."

"Until Johnny marries," Selena said, casting a look of dislike at her mother.

"You have not met my son, Miss Beck." Levanah turned to Cat, including her in the conversation. "Johnny has not yet settled down, I fear. He has rushed off and taken a commission in the Royal Air Force. Now he cannot wait for us to go to war with somebody or other! I had hoped he would be able to join us tonight but he is far too busy flying that new airplane about."

"The Tiger Moth," Leah confirmed. "Such a pretty name for such an ugly little machine."

"Leah is a pretty name," said Sigrid, gazing into space dreamily.

"That was impertinent," Leah said.

"Was it, Grandmother? I'm so sorry." The girl gave a wide mirthless smile. At her side Margot giggled shrilly, her narrow eyes gleaming.

There is a sickness here, Cat thought. *A sickness of the spirit that hangs like a foul odor in the air. It has not touched Giles or Selena, but those four are tainted.*

She leaned back in her chair, sipping her sherry, watching them from under her eyelashes. There was, now that she had leisure to observe them, a tension in those four. It manifested itself in little, subtle ways; in the closeness in which Sigrid and Margot sat, in the dark shadows under Leah's sunken eyes, in the restless plucking of Levanah's thin fingers at her chiffon skirt. She wondered if any of them had begun to realize that they had been bound.

"It's odd," said Margot, "but Miss Beck fits in here like one of us."

"I certainly hope we've made her welcome," Leah said, "and that you two have both behaved yourselves at school."

"We behave very well," Sigrid said demurely. "Don't we, Miss Beck?"

Cat nodded. In the few weeks since term had begun the girls had been punctual, polite and industrious. In all honesty she had not been able to find fault with their behavior. Only in their sly smiles and furtive glances did she discern corruption.

"I'd better drive over and see if my mother is ready," Giles said. "It always takes her forever to get ready to go anywhere."

Cat had a sudden, irrational desire to say, "Go with him, Selena. Go with him and don't come back."

She remained silent as he rose, stretching, and patted his wife on the shoulder.

"With any luck I'll be back within the hour with the old people," he told them.

He had scarcely gone when Selena rounded on her mother, her cheeks as red as her hair.

"Do you have to be so uncivil to my husband whenever we visit?" she inquired icily.

"As a member of the family he must be prepared to endure a little teasing," Levanah countered.

"You can scarcely regard him as a member of the family when he has abandoned the name of Falcon—"

"To which he was never entitled in the first place, his father being a bastard." Levanah completed Leah's sentence.

"And do you have to keep using that word?" Selena demanded. "In front of a stranger!"

"I was born bastard myself," Cat said levelly. "I've never known who my father was and my mother abandoned me."

"How dreadful for you!" Selena began, but Levanah interrupted, a harsh note in her voice, "Who reared you then?"

"An old aunt," Cat said. "She told me something of my mother and of my grandmother too. My grandmother killed herself, poor soul. My mother went back to her own people after I was born. When I was a child I used to promise myself that one day I'd find her and ask her to tell me the truth."

A sudden gust of wind sent a shower of sparks down the chimney. Levanah, her eyes curiously blank, said, her voice still harsh, "Perhaps she never wanted you."

"But she must have cared for me a little," Cat said. Her own eyes, brilliantly green, were fixed steadily upon Levanah's white face. "She left a ring for me. I wear it on special occasions."

"A ring?" Levanah's voice was an echo.

Cat drew the moonstone from her skirt pocket and fitted it onto the index finger of her right hand. As she displayed it there was silence for a moment. Then Leah, craning her neck, cried out, " But that is Beth's ring! What is Miss Beck doing with my sister's ring?"

"My mother left it with me," Cat said.

"There must be hundreds of moonstone rings," Levanah said.

"That was my sister's ring," Leah said obstinately. "My mother left each of her daughters a ring. Beth had the moonstone. After she killed herself I kept the ring for Levanah. I gave it to her when she was a girl, but I've not seen it for years."

"My mother left it with me," Cat said. Her voice shook with excited terror. "She left it with me. She left something else with me too, though she never knew it at the time, for she refused to look at me after I was born."

"I don't understand." Selena was looking from one to the other in confusion. "I don't understand any of this!"

"My mother bequeathed a sign to me, a mark," Cat said breathlessly.

She stood up then, lifting her long skirt, displaying above the top of her silk stocking the purple crescent.

"There have always been certain women in every generation of Falcons who bore the devil's kiss," she said. "My grandmother bore the mark; so did my mother. Aunt Cat told me."

"Aunt Cat? But Cousin Wenna's mother was—Levanah, this young woman is claiming to be—but that's not possible! Levanah, explain it to me," Leah said thickly.

"Isn't it clear enough for your agile brain?" Levanah asked. "This young woman is claiming, quite truthfully and correctly, to be my daughter."

"*I'm* your daughter," Selena said. "Johnny is your son and I'm your daughter. Miss Beck is—"

"My bastard daughter," Levanah said with forced calm.

"You left me with old Aunt Cat, and I always wanted to meet you, to ask you why you didn't want me," Cat said.

"If I'd known about the mark," Levanah said slowly, "I'd have wanted you."

"To train me as you were trained?" Cat asked. "Where were you trained? Who showed you how to use your power?"

"You know about these things?" Levanah asked.

"From a lady who took care of me after Aunt Cat died," Cat said. "She taught me how to use the power. She taught me how to use it wisely."

"She means to hurt us," Sigrid said.

She and Margot were huddled together, and though the younger girl still looked bewildered the elder had a dawning comprehension in her face.

"She has begun to hurt us," Margot said. "I dreamed of a tree on the night she came. A tree with leaves that smelled like vinegar."

"The old curse tree that killed Willow Falcon," Leah said. "My mother told me of it."

"That has nothing to do with anything," Selena said impatiently. "Mother, are you saying that Miss Beck is my—my half sister? That you had a baby before you married Father?"

"When I sent you away to London," Leah said slowly, "you went up to Wales, to Saron. You stayed with Aunt Cat for a long time, almost a year. It was then that you had the child, wasn't it?"

"I told the old woman to put it in an orphanage," Levanah said. "I left the moonstone to defray expenses. How was I to know that Aunt Cat would disregard my wishes?"

"I was told a little about you all," Cat said. "I knew that one day I'd come to Marie Regina."

"To enjoy a loving reunion with a long-lost parent? How touching!" Levanah said.

"I wanted to see you for myself and I wanted to ask you who my father was," Cat said. "A child has the right to know that."

"Why should you?" Levanah said, a bitter humor twisting her pale mouth. "Why should you know your father's name when I never did?"

"Mother!" Selena's voice was horrified. Margot giggled shrilly again.

"I didn't learn my own father's name until I went seeking," Levanah said, "and I have never known who fathered my first child."

"A disgrace to the family name," Leah said, rocking back and forth in satisfaction. "I always knew you'd bring shame and scandal."

"The family name?" Levanah threw back her red head and laughed. "A fine name, isn't it? Falcon! The Falcons of Kingsmead flaunting their iniquities for the village to wonder at."

"We had a proud name, an honorable name," said Leah.

"Proud? Honorable? Why, the first Falcon got his knighthood for stealing monastery land," Levanah said scornfully. "One of the earliest Falcon wives was drowned as a witch down in the village pond. There's an honorable beginning!"

"That was centuries ago." Selena was almost in tears.

"And what makes you think we've improved since?" Levanah inquired. "What leads you to suppose that the years have gentled us? Do you think the evil stopped when the land was gained and the witch was wed? Not so! It rolled like a snowball down the centuries and grew bigger as it went."

"This is fun," Margot said, and bounced up and down a little.

"I'm a Falcon too," said Cat. Her voice was defiant but her heart thudded nervously.

"Then welcome!" Levanah spread thin fingers. "Welcome to the illustrious family, my dear. Your ancestors are all up there, tidily tucked into their frames. They'd greet you if they could! And you can be very proud of them. Regina Falcon, for instance—the king's whore, but she won a peerage for *her* bastard. None of us has done as well since! And here is her bastard—Lord Charles Falcon. They say he was a slayer of women, and a sucker of blood, and rides the common with hellhounds at his back."

"That's enough!" Leah shouted, her face working. Levanah ignored her and went on.

"There's Lord Edward Falcon. He drove his wife to suicide and two of his daughters had to run away in order to marry. And there is Mair, his grandson's wife. She ran away too and bore twin daughters, Catrin and Saran."

"And Catrin became old Aunt Cat and Saran lay down under the apple trees for a traveling man," Cat said.

"And the child born was my own mother," Leah said. "You never knew her, either of you, so don't dare to say a word against her. She never used her power for evil, but loved my father until the day of her death."

"So you think the evil ended there?" Levanah inquired. "It went underground for a while, that's all. You made certain it revived, didn't you?"

"I want to go home," Selena said tearfully. "I don't want to listen to any of this."

"Why not?" her mother demanded. "What gives you the right to live in ignorance of what we are?"

"You kept her in ignorance," Leah interposed. "Her and Johnny."

"It was a mistake," Levanah said. "I tried to keep them clean and proud, and they repaid me miserably, for Johnny is still unwed and Selena threw herself away on Giles Shaw!"

"Leave Giles out of it," Selena sobbed.

"I wish we could!" Levanah retorted. Her yellow eyes were blazing with temper, and her lips were tightly compressed. "I wish that neither he nor his father had ever been spawned, and Aunt Leah has more reason to wish that than any of us, for it was her own husband who fathered her sister's child!"

"So I was right to come." Cat felt a little sick. "I was right to come to try and stop the evil."

"She has bound us," Sigrid said, and continued, "I knew something had happened. Margot and I both felt it on the night she arrived. Nothing has gone right since. Even Witch's Dower felt odd when I was there the other afternoon. It was—empty. She has bound us, Levanah."

"Bound what?" Selena asked. "What is all this talk of binding?"

"To stop us from doing—" Margot began and yelped as Sigrid kicked her on the shin.

"From doing what?" Selena demanded. "What have you done that needs to be bound?"

"The witch mark," said Leah. "Have you never

thought about it, Selena? Have you and Johnny never wondered about it?"

"It's an old story," the girl said uneasily, dabbing her eyes. "It's a birthmark with lots of silly superstitions that have grown up around it."

"You're a fool," Levanah said. "You and Johnny are both fools not to have realized long ago that the old ways seldom die, and there are powers of which you know nothing. I was born with the mark and so could use my power to draw in others. Not you and Johnny. I kept you both out of it."

"Because it gave you more pleasure to corrupt Mary's children," Leah said. "You were always jealous of Mary."

"Why should I be jealous of a girl who had the whole district whispering about her unnatural taste in women friends?"

"She was my mother," Sigrid objected. "You ought not to say such things about my mother."

"And my daughter," said Leah.

"As soft and stupid as you are greedy and stupid," Levanah flashed. To Cat she said mockingly, "So you came down here to bind the evil that we do, did you? But you don't even know the beginning, my dear. You don't know how it began with Leah."

"You swore you'd never tell," Leah said gaspingly.

"Let them all know," Levanah said. There was a recklessness in her white face. "It began when Leah, my darling Aunt Leah, took charge of this household after her parents died. There were three sisters and two brothers and Aunt Leah, being the eldest, wished to control the rest. Tell them, Aunt. Tell them how you stopped Edith and Beth from marrying. Tell them how when you learned your brother John was impotent and your brother Price was about to be-

come the father of a bastard you sent Price off to
South Africa and bribed his mistress to marry John
and pretend that her child was his seed."

"She repaid me ill, did Grace Finn," said Leah
sullenly. "She was a common piece of impudence,
but she was carrying Price's child. He never knew
about it and I packed him off to South Africa before he'd a chance to find out. And I told John I'd
find him a nice wife who would help him to become
a man. Grace was pleased to become Lady Falcon and
John believed that Teddy was his son. It could have
been perfect."

"What happened?" Sigrid asked.

"I'll tell you," said Levanah with pleasure. "Aunt
Leah was married to a man called Paul Simmons. He
eloped with Grace, and after they'd left she discovered that her own sister, Edith, was with child by
him too."

"It broke John's heart," said Leah. "He never
mentioned Grace again and soon afterward he was
killed in a riding accident. I reared the boy, Teddy,
with my own daughter, Mary. Edith went to live at
Whittle Farm and brought up her son, Caleb, there."

"Beth had a child too," said Cat.

"Michael Shaw's baby," Leah said. "He went back
to his wife, not knowing Beth was pregnant. Levanah was born and my sister committed suicide."

"Tell them why," Levanah taunted. "Tell them
how you lied to her, pretending that Michael Shaw
was dead, and how she killed herself in grief and despair. Tell them how you reared me along with your
own daughter and Teddy. Little Levanah being
cared for by her kind Aunt Leah!"

"I'll tell them how you went to Witch's Dower,"

Leah grated, "and set up your filthy rituals there, and dragged Mary into your wickedness."

"Wickedness! In those days I didn't even know the meaning of the word," Levanah said. "I found a portrait of my mother and a crystal ball in the cottage and Cousin Cal made a little woodland god for me. We lit candles and danced, and there was no evil in it. The evil was in your own mind, Aunt Leah. You wouldn't listen to anything I had to say."

"I sent you away," Leah said. "I cut you out like a cancer and sent you to London. A little humbling was what you needed."

"The best-laid plans can go astray," Levanah said. "You don't know, do you, what happened when I went to London?"

"You met my father?"

"I was employed as a companion to a rich widow," Levanah said. "What Aunt Leah didn't know was that my employer was a member of a very powerful black lodge. I was initiated into it and I learned quickly. Oh, I learned very quickly."

"My father," Cat said tensely. "Who was my father?"

"Grand Magus of the lodge, of course," Levanah said. "Oh, I never knew his real name. He came and went by night when the moon was waning, and he wore the devil's horns and a dark cloak."

"I don't believe any of this," Selena whispered. "I don't believe it."

"Would you believe that when I'd learned everything that those people could teach me there was a most unfortunate accident?" her mother asked softly. "The whole house burnt to the ground and every member of the group killed? Does that surprise you?"

"Oh no. Oh no," Selena moaned softly.

"I escaped—quite miraculously," said Levanah. "I went up to the farm in Wales and my baby was born there. I never wanted her, but I left the moon-stone to pay Aunt Catrin for her trouble and the other things—the crystal, and Beth's picture, and the wooden lob—I had no use for them anymore. And I came back here. I came back to my dear Aunt Leah."

"And went on with your evil," said Cat. "But no more! You'll do nothing more to hurt anybody."

"Because you have bound us?" Levanah smiled again, her eyes foxlike under the fringe of light red hair. "Do you think your arts are equal to mine? You're a fool, my dear bastard daughter! And I've been a fool too. Had I known you bore the mark I'd have kept you with me, and trained you up in the way I wanted you to go."

"But why evil?" Cat asked helplessly. "Why evil?"

"Because nobody ever got anywhere by being good," Levanah said. "Beth was good and trusting and she died, and I made up my mind long ago that what the world didn't give me I would take, with both hands."

"That's insane," Selena whispered. "You must be insane."

"Perhaps it runs in the family," Levanah mocked. "If so, then you are part of it, for you are Falcon too."

"You can't stop us," Margot said to Cat. "You can't do anything, and if you ever tell nobody will believe you."

Overhead the humming of a light aircraft sounded in the silence that had descended on the great hall.

"This is 1936," Selena cried out. "Men fly in airplanes, listen to the wireless, film moving pictures! The old ways are dead."

"Not dead, my dear. Just sleeping for a while," Levanah said.

"She's right. You are insane," Cat said slowly.

"I'm a Falcon," Levanah told her. "We Falcons have always taken what we wanted. Cheer up! Now that you've met us you'll grow to love us all quite soon. We'll drink a toast to our reunion. A toast to the family!"

Her voice was gay and a weird excitement had robbed her features of their sharpness. Only her eyes gleamed golden still and her slender neck was arched as if she were a vixen waiting for the rising moon. As she stood, wineglass in hand, under the chandelier she was like the spirit of the house, the fulfillment of every grief and joy that had ever left its imprint on stone, and wood, and drifting fold of gray tapestry. The others were drawn toward her as if she held the web of their natures in her thin hands.

Johnny, at the controls of the Tiger Moth, looked down at the bulk of the old house below. He had landed a little time previously on the field beyond the rose garden. The flat ground, the bright moonlight, had made little demand upon his skill. It was months since he had been home, and this visit had been a spur of the moment decision. His mother and old Aunt Leah set great store by this anniversary. It would please them if he arrived unexpectedly, and he was confident that the station commander, being a decent sort, would turn a blind eye if one of his training planes was borrowed by young Lord Falcon.

So Johnny, having landed, had run lightly through the fringe of deer park that surrounded the lawns and rose garden, and entered the house through the French windows that opened into the drawing room. Treading softly, his face anticipating their pleased surprise, he had pushed the hall door a few inches wide and seen Cat, the girl whose green eyes haunted his dreams and for whom he had looked in vain.

Cat, his half sister! His mother smiling as she talked of murder and evil and strange powers. Aunt Leah, half-afraid, half-gloating over old sins. Selena, terrified, yet with a growing fascination in the gray eyes fixed on her relatives. The sly mirth in their young faces.

Everything in his world was dark and twisted, and his limbs were shackled with horror. His life was a mockery of every good thing he had ever believed, and even his love for Cat had become something ugly and unnatural. He had left as quietly as he had come, though he had no memory of having quitted the house or having run back across the dark lawns. He was in the cockpit again, aiming for the moon, and then the landscape fanned out below him.

He could see the broad ribbon of river that bisected the main road and turned Marie Regina into a cross. He could see the spire of the church and the whispering woods, pointing their branches up toward him, and the jagged ruins of the ancient monastery high on the hill. This was his world and the world of his family for four centuries, but the world was false and cruel, and nothing was as it had been in his innocent years.

The headlights of a car snaked over the bridge, heading toward Kingsmead. His home had been a gracious house, built to endure, but it had endured too long and grown corrupt, its walls stained with the sins of its inhabitants.

"Victory will not come until a falcon rides upon a moth," he called aloud, and the familiar saying had meaning and coherence, and a strange kind of beauty, for he, last of the male Falcons, could set things right.

"God bless you, Cat," he called to his sister-sweetheart, and dipped a wing in salute before he climbed again beneath the moon and arched his aircraft at the vaulted roof. He fell then like an angel, the petrol tanks exploding as he ripped through slate and plaster and ribbed wood, tearing out the heart of the great hall as he plummeted to the stone floor.

Flames seared the air and the ancient tapestries billowed out to greet the fiery towers that rose as high as the screams of the dying women. Wine and blood mingled with smashed bone and wood and splintered glass. Burning metal was flung up the staircase and little streams of fire licked the wainscoting and ate at the carpet laid along the gallery. In the heat there was no sound save the high-pitched screaming of old Leah, who lay, back and legs crushed, near to the others. Of those others only Levanah had survived that first, terrible impact. She had dragged herself to her feet and for a moment she stood quite still, her face bewildered like a child whose toys are being wantonly destroyed. Then a finger of flame tugged at the petrol-splashed chiffon of her gown, and she was no longer a human being but a pillar of fire that writhed and moaned and twisted as the dying Leah watched.

The sky was lit by the glow of fire and the moon struggled through a veil of blood to illumine the scene below. There were people running from the servants' quarters with mouths agape, and the screeching of brakes as Giles drew his car to a shuddering stop.

Down by the river a falcon, perched high on a tree above Witch's Dower, left her branch and hovered for an instant, black wings stretched under the silver moon. She had no knowledge of good or evil, or of love and hate, and time was only a dream dreamed by those who could not measure seasons by the calling of the wind. But she set a course for the south, beak pointed into the future, every instinct telling her that something had come to an end.

And when she had gone the woods were tranquil again and all the night creatures were still.

Catherine Darby's
The Falcon Saga

A series of brilliant historical gothic romances by one of England's foremost authors.